# Someone to See that I CARE

SOMEONE SERIES BOOK 6

# Someone to See that I CARE

## ROBERT LEWIS

4 Horsemen
Publications, Inc.

*Published By: 4 Horsemen Publications, Inc.*

*4 Horsemen Publications, Inc.*
*PO Box 417*
*Sylva, NC 28779*
*4horsemenpublications.com*
*info@4horsemenpublications.com*

*Cover & Typesetting by Autumn Skye*
*Cover Image by Mark E. Hersh*
*Edited by Kris Cotter*



*Library of Congress Control Number: 2025939640*

*Paperback ISBN-13: 979-8-8232-0912-0*
*Hardcover ISBN-13: 979-8-8232-0913-7*
*Audiobook ISBN-13: 979-8-8232-0915-1*
*Ebook ISBN-13: 979-8-8232-0914-4*

# Dedication

**T**HIS BOOK, AS with all my books, is dedicated to my beloved mother and father, Dolores C. Lewis and Robert O. Lewis. I also dedicate this to my brother Harry Lewis, who doesn't miss an opportunity to brag about my writing to his friends and strangers. Of course, I have to include a dedication to the diva Bonita, who took me for plenty of mini-walks and demanded plenty of snuggles and attention while writing this.

To my Bonita Boys, Randy, Chris, William, Berto, Rodney, Brian, and Kalvin, and my Diva Duo, Amanda and Donna for all the love and support they have given me over the years. To Thomas Gilchrist for making me smile when I needed it and being one of my biggest cheerleaders.

I would be remiss if I did not include a special dedication to Morgan Moreau and Kate Jenkins for their encouragement and help keeping me insane while writing this.

# NOTE FROM THE AUTHOR.

This book occurs during the same time period as *Someone to Marry* and *Someone to Shadow*, and is the conclusion of the *Someone Series*. It contains spoilers for those books.

# Table of Contents

# 1

# SHOWER THOUGHTS

**W**ITH ONE HAND pressed to the cold tile, and head bowed, Alex wished the water that cascaded over him had the power to carry his shame and guilt down the drain with the other filth he washed from his body. With his thirst for prestige and fame, he had risen to the so-called top of the adult film industry by hurting the people he cared about.

He looked up into the spray, pondering his choices. *No one will work with me, much less talk to me.* He leaned against the shower wall and sank down. *I get hit by a car and wake up in a hospital room with my ex-fiancé and his new boyfriend at my bedside. Now I'm recovering in his aunt's mansion.*

Lexi had taken him in when she found out he was staying in hotels after moving out of the condo he once shared with his ex-fiancé, Cameron. She didn't give him much of a choice, taking him directly from the hospital to her mansion. She told him to make himself at home, but her place felt no more like home than the condo he had shared with Cameron.

Water dripped down his body as Alex pushed himself up to his feet. *When have I ever felt at home some place?* The answer to that question hurt more than he expected it to. It was never officially his home, but it was nonetheless. It was where he felt safe and loved. It was where he had found love and lost it.

*"What do you want to do today?" Alex asked, plopping onto Owen's bed.*

*Owen huffed irritably, "Dude, I just made the bed."*

*"Lighten up." Alex threw a pillow at him. "Uncle Terry is out of town for another day. Live a little. Have some fun."*

*Owen threw the pillow back, hitting Alex in the face. "Get up. We've got chores to do."*

*"I got a chore you can do." Alex grabbed his crotch.*

*Owen walked away. "Handle that yourself, but not in my bed."*

*"Owen!" Alex jumped out of the bed and chased after him. "Come on! I'm bored. Let's go do something fun!"*

*Owen stopped and turned around suddenly. Alex slammed into him, sending the two crashing to the floor, a tangle of limbs. "Get off me!" Owen shouted, trying to get out from under Alex.*

*"Quit squirming and I will!" Alex ordered, struggling to get off his friend.*

*The two ended up face to face, Alex looking down into his friend's big brown eyes and Owen gazing up into his friend's mischievous blue eyes. With their bodies pressed close, they could not mistake the other's arousal with the hard press of their cocks into each other.*

*Alex brushed the hair from Owen's face. It was no secret that he wanted his best friend and the feeling was mutual. The only reason they hadn't acted upon their youthful carnal desires was because of Alex's Uncle Terry. When he saw the unmistakable look in their eyes when Alex came over and met Owen for the first time, he quickly laid down the law.*

*"Get off me." Owen's low voice filled with denied lust. "You know the rules."*

*Alex smiled impishly. "We're both eighteen and high school graduates as of last week." Alex brushed his lips over Owen's. "The rules don't apply anymore."*

*"Alex." Owen put his arms around him. "The rules still apply." Owen rolled them over so he was on top. "Now, behave." He stood up. "Now get up and help me clean the house."*

*With a groan, Alex got up. "Why? Uncle Terry won't be back for another day." He scrunched up his face in thought. "Where did he go, anyways? Did he say?"*

*"You straighten up in here, and I'll tackle the kitchen," Owen instructed, purposely ignoring the question. "Do you want pizza for dinner?"*

*Alex stretched out on the sofa. "Yeah."*

*"What are you doing?" Owen asked with his hands on his hips. "Get up and clean this room."*

*Alex yawned. "What does it look like?"*

*"It looks like you're trying to drive me crazy." Owen huffed. "If you're going to stay here while your mother is*

*visiting your sister, then you're going to help me keep the place clean."*

*Alex stood up and stretched. "Fine. I'll go back to my house."*

*"Tell me." Owen crossed his arms. With poorly restrained anger, he asked, "Did your mother leave you any food? Money for food? Is the power on at your house? The water?"*

*Hurt, Alex answered the question without answering it, "I'll straighten up in here."*

*"Alex." Owen crossed the room and put a hand on his friend's arm. "I didn't mean to…" His words were lost on his tongue. "I'm sorry. I really am."*

*Alex forced a smile. "It's okay. I get it. My sister needs her. I don't." His smile brightened. "I have you and Uncle Terry."*

*"You'll always have me." Owen pulled him into a hug. "I'll always be here for you."*

*With imploring eyes, Alex looked deep into his friend's eyes. "I know." Two simple words, but they spoke volumes. They were filled with years of hurt and disappointment. They were filled with love and appreciation.*

*Alex leaned in for a kiss.*

*Owen pulled away.*

*"I need to tell you something." Owen looked everywhere but at Alex. He worried his bottom lip. After a tense moment of silence, he said, "I'm leaving." He looked at Alex. "I was accepted to State." Owen gave him a sad smile. "I leave for school in two months."*

*Alex plastered on a fake smile. "That's great." He moved closer to Owen, but Owen moved away. "We still*

have the summer? And you'll be back to visit and for hol-idays? Right?"

"Alex." There was no mistaking the pain in Owen's voice. "I..."

Alex took Owen back in his arms. "I don't care if it is a lie, just tell me yes."

"It's not a lie." Owen put his arms around Alex. "Things are just going to be complicated."

Holding Owen close, Alex asked, "When are things not complicated?"

"Alex," Owen said softly before pressing his lips to Alex's.

Alex deepened the tentative kiss. He held onto Owen, never wanting to let go of him or the moment. Their tongues danced awkwardly about. Owen held him tighter. Alex pushed his hands up under Owen's shirt, needing to touch him, to feel his skin. He felt Owen jump at his touch, then relax into his arms.

"We shouldn't do this," Owen moaned, pulling up the hem of Alex's shirt. Alex reluctantly let go so Owen could pull his shirt off. "This is a bad idea."

Alex pulled Owen's shirt off and tossed it to the side. Pulling Owen back to him, he said, "I have a lot of ideas for you and none of them are bad."

Alex kissed him, soft and sensual. His cock throbbed in his shorts. He could feel Owen's excitement pressing into him through their shorts. He ran his hands down Owen's back, stopping at the small of Owen's back before growing bold and moving lower. He squeezed Owen's tight butt. They both moaned.

Trying to catch his breath, Owen gasped, "Alex."

*"I love how you moan my name." Alex teased with a kiss. He fumbled with the front of Owen's shorts. "They make this look so much easier in porn."*

*Owen pushed Alex's hands away. Popping open the front of his shorts, he said, "This isn't porn; it's real life." He let his shorts fall to the floor, leaving him in his tight white briefs. Stepping out of his shorts, he easily popped open the top of Alex's shorts. Shoving them down Alex's hips, he laughed, "Why aren't you wearing any underwear?"*

*"Why are you still in yours?" Alex dropped to his knees. He smiled up at Owen. He pulled the briefs down, freeing Owen's excitement. Owen lifted one foot, then the other. Alex ran his hands up the sides of Owen's legs to his hips. "That's better."*

*Alex stroked Owen. He was mesmerized by the feel of the hard yet soft flesh in his grip. He kissed the tip. He smiled up at Owen, then opened his mouth to take the head of his cock. He swirled his tongue over the crown, savoring his first taste of man in his mouth.*

*"Oh, Alex," Owen moaned, putting a hand on Alex's shoulder.*

*Alex took more of Owen's cock into his mouth, then pulled back slowly. Alex moaned, enjoying the slide of a hard dick across his lips. A quick slide of his tongue over the crown, and Alex was sliding Owen back into his mouth. Tightening his grip on Alex's shoulder, Owen gasped.*

*Alex's hand went around to feel Owen's tight, youthful rear. He guided Owen, pushing and pulling his best friend in and out of his mouth. Alex pulled Owen deeper into his mouth, pushing Owen against the back of his throat. He pulled back slowly, feeling every vein and bump brush over his lips.*

*Owen's hand ran through Alex's blond hair. He pulled Alex onto his cock while moving his hips forward. "Alex." Owen's voice trembled when he spoke. "Oh, God, Alex."*

*He pushed Alex off, leaned down, and kissed him. Alex fell back, and they ended up with Owen on top. Owen kissed down Alex's slender, smooth body. He paused right before the head of Alex's cock. He looked up at Alex's lust-addled face. He smiled, then licked down Alex's length.*

*"You fucking tease," Alex growled.*

*Owen laughed softly then licked his way up. He flicked his tongue over the crown, causing Alex to let out a growl of frustration. Wrapping his hand around Alex's shaft, he lifted Alex's cock up, then took Alex into his mouth with an unadulterated carnal satisfaction.*

*"Yes, Owen," Alex moaned, throwing his head back. He ran a hand through Owen's short, black hair. "Suck me, Owen. Suck me." He pushed his hips up into Owen's suckling mouth. "Yeah, take that dick, boy."*

*Owen pulled off Alex. "What's with the cheesy porn talk?"*

*"It sounds hot in porn." Alex laughed. "Let me suck you while you suck me."*

*Owen smiled. "Anything to keep you from saying any more cheesy porn lines."*

*Alex turned on his side, while Owen maneuvered his body so they were cock to mouth. Alex wasted no time engulfing Owen's cock back into the warm wetness of his mouth. He slipped an arm around Owen and grabbed his ass. He ventured a finger between Owen's cheeks. He brushed the soft skin.*

*Owen gasped around Alex's cock. His body went rigid. His cheeks clenched, trapping Alex's finger. Alex's cock*

muffled his mewling cry as his cock shot rapid fire into Alex's mouth. He furiously sucked Alex. A second later, Alex let out a similar muffled cry, and Owen's mouth was filled with Alex's load.

The two continued to nurse on each other's spent cocks until Owen finally pulled off and shoved Alex off his cock. "Sensitive," he said, exhaling deeply.

"I'll give you sensitive." Alex covered Owen's body with his. They kissed, tongues swirling around one another. "I like the taste of me on your lips," he teased before rolling off and lying beside Owen. "We need lube so I can fuck you."

Breathing heavily, Owen responded, "I have lube, and I'm fucking you."

"Oh, yeah?" Alex asked, rolling on to his side. He danced his fingers over Owen's chest. "Well, go get it."

Pushing Alex's hand away, Owen stood up. "Get dressed. We need to get this place cleaned up." He offered his hand to Alex. "I'm not having Terry come home to a mess and the smell of sex."

"Do you really expect me to function after learning the joys of your mouth?" Alex took Owen's hand and pulled himself up so they stood face to face. "You were my first, you know that?"

Owen pecked his lips. "Mine too." He ran a hand through Alex's messy hair. "Now, if you want to be my second, get dressed and clean up this room."

"Okay." Alex returned the peck. His tone grew somber. "Promise me that you'll always be there for me."

Owen pressed his forehead to Alex's. "Always and forever. No matter what."

With one hand pressed against the shower wall and his other hand flying over his dick, Alex exploded. The evidence of his orgasm slowly ran down the tile wall. His chest heaved. Regaining his senses, he took the shower spray and washed away the documentation of his momentary bliss.

*There's nothing left for me here except embarrassment and shame.* Alex turned off the water. Stepping out of the shower, he dried himself off. *That bastard Owen owes me something after what he did to me and my family.*

Alex grabbed his phone. After five minutes of taps on the screen, his flight was booked. *I'll be gone before Lexi is back.* Alex started throwing his clothes into a bag. *I'll be one less thing for her to worry about.*

Slipping into comfortable clothes, he ordered a ride to the airport. He hefted his bag over his shoulder, wincing at a lingering pain from the hit-and-run. He made his way downstairs to the front of the mansion. *I'll text her when I land; that way she won't worry.* He laughed to himself. *After three years out here, the only person who'd worry about me is my ex-fiancé's aunt. How pathetic.*

# LATE NIGHT VISITORS

"**C**OMING!" OWEN SHOUTED at the pounding on his door. Stumbling out of his room, he made his way to the front door, turning lights on as he went. "It's three in the fucking morning," he muttered, rubbing the sleep from his eyes. He checked through a nearby window to make sure the security lights were on. He thought they were a frivolous investment at the time, but was now grateful Terry had made him get them installed.

Looking through the peephole, Owen silently cursed when he saw the familiar uniformed figure standing on his front porch. *This asshole again.* Owen cut his eyes at the pounding on the door. *Let's see what he wants this time.*

Owen purposely took his time opening the locks. Opening the door, he glared at the smug police officer. "Why are you here, Stewie?"

"That's Officer Stuart Jackson to you," he snarled back.

Unintimidated, Owen crossed his arms over his old tee. "That's why are you trespassing on my property again for no reason," Owen paused, smiling with malicious enjoyment when he said, "Stewie?"

"It's not really your property, now is it?" Stuart commented, puffing out his chest.

Refusing to back down, Owen smiled smugly. "Really? Because that's not what it says on the deed, now does it? Now either tell me why you're here or get the fuck off my property."

"It would be a shame if you turned up missing." Stuart took a step forward. "With you living all the way out here, where no one can hear anything, it could be months before we noticed you were gone."

Owen grinned. "Could you repeat that?" He motioned over to the camera in the corner with his head. "I don't think the cameras caught all that."

"Whatever." Stuart stepped back. "I'm here because we received a noise complaint."

Owen rolled his eyes. "You just said I live where no one can hear anything."

"I did not," Stuart sputtered out. "Anyways, I'll let you go with a warning this time. Keep it down. If I have to come out here again, I'm writing you a ticket."

Owen smiled triumphantly. "I'll make sure to bring a copy of that recording to court with me." Frowning, Owen snapped, "Now get off my property before I call my attorney. He's not as nice as me when he's woken up at three in the morning."

"Fuck you, Owen." Stuart stormed off the porch to his patrol car.

Waving at him, Owen called after him, "Have a good night!" He watched the patrol car pull off before he went back in. Locking the door, he mumbled, "Asshole."

He ran a hand over the picture of Terry he kept by the door. "Your family is fucking psycho, you know that?" Closing his eyes, he chewed his lower lip. "It wasn't supposed to be like this. No one was ever supposed to find out our secret."

Owen made his way back to his bedroom, turning lights off as he went. He would send a copy of the video to his attorney in the morning, then endure the scathing judgmental looks when he headed into town to file yet another complaint.

He hadn't asked for this. Any of it. He was too young to not be off chasing his dreams, making mistakes, and memories. Instead, he was a young man forced to grow up too soon and take on responsibilities he wasn't prepared for. Now he was unfairly being cruelly judged for it all.

Turning off the bedside lamp, he settled back down into bed. Closing his eyes, he tried to release his anger. He tossed and turned, hearing the malicious whispers said loud enough for him to hear and the vicious comments shouted at him by those brave enough to let their homophobia show in his head.

*"Gold digging, cocksucker!"*

*"Thieving whore!"*

*"Slut!"*

*"Filthy faggot!"*

*"Ass licking parasite!"*

Rolling onto his back, Owen opened his eyes to stare out into the darkness. He wouldn't let them drive him from his home. He and Alex had endured enough of their childish hate when they were in school. Then, he had Alex to lean on. Now he had to stand on his own.

Closing his eyes again, he begged for sleep to whisk him away for a few short hours of peace. His mind continued to race, bringing up hurtful memory after hurtful memory. The voices continued to echo in his head. Through watery eyes, he checked the time. It was five in the morning.

Pounding on the front door startled him. *What the fuck does he want now?!* Owen pulled himself out of bed. "There's no point in trying to get any sleep tonight," he said aloud, swinging his legs over the bed. With a groan, he started for the front door, flipping lights on again.

Whoever it was on the other side was pounding on the door again. Harder. Angrier. It gave Owen pause, but he refused to be intimidated in his own home. "I'm coming!" he shouted angrily. He checked to ensure the security lights were on. He peered through the peephole only to see the back of a blond guy's head.

He shouted through the door, "What do you want?" Owen froze when the man turned around. He started unlocking the door. *Let's see what he wants.* Given their history, he knew it probably wasn't a good idea, but he couldn't rightfully deny the man on his front porch entry. It wasn't like he could ever deny him anything.

Opening the door, his voice was a blend of anger, hurt, and longing. "Hey, Alex."
"Hi, Uncle Owen," Alex said with pure malice.

# NOT SO WARM WELCOME HOME

**A**LEX WATCHED THE hesitant smile on Owen's face falter. His words had done what he had intended, hurt Owen. "Did you miss me?"

"I did until you opened your mouth," Owen sniped back. "May I ask what I owe the pleasure of your visit," Owen emphasized his next words, "after three years?"

Alex hoisted his bag up onto his shoulder. He winced at its weight. "It was time for me to get out of California and come back home."

"Well, your name is on the deed with mine." Owen stepped aside to let Alex inside. "Whatever problems you're going to cause for me, I'd appreciate it if you'd hold off until tomorrow. I'm too tired to deal with any of your shit."

Stepping in, Alex looked around. "The place looks nice." He dropped his bag on the sofa. "Where can I lay down at? I'm exhausted. I've been up all night. I need to get some sleep."

"You put your bag on it," Owen answered, locking the doors. Turning to face Alex, he found it hard to be mean to him. Hard, but not impossible. "There's only one bed, and it's mine. You get the couch."

Alex slumped his shoulders in defeat. "Look, can we save all the hostilities until after I've gotten some sleep? When I wake up, I'll go into town, buy a bed for me, and have it delivered."

"Someone in town come here?" Owen laughed. "I have to drive to another town to get groceries, thanks to those bitches, Danielle and Krystal."

Alex tensed back up. His voice grew threatening. "Watch what you say about my mom and sister."

"What I say about them?" Owen threw his head back in laughter. "What about what they say about me? What about all the problems they have been causing me since Terry died?" Owen's chest began heaving with anger. Pointing at the door, he snarled, "Stewie comes at least three times a week at all hours of the night with some bogus complaint! I can't even go into town without being called names behind my back and to my face! Not to mention what they say about me online!"

Owen took a step closer to Alex. "They have had my water and electricity cut off multiple times. They have tried to have me evicted from my own home. Anytime I leave the property, I run the risk of being pulled over by Stewie or one of his asshole cop buddies! The only reason they stopped arresting me was because I got a lawyer to threaten them with a lawsuit! So excuse me if I call them bitches! It is the nicest thing I can say about either of them."

"You're kidding right?" Alex looked at Owen in disbelief. He reached out and put a hand on Owen's shoulder. "I know they were upset about the will, but it's been three years."

Owen almost let his guard down with Alex's tender touch. "Why are you really here?! Are you here to help them force me out of my home?! Because now that you're here, you can buy me out or we can sell it! That way I can get out of this hell and cut ties with you and your psycho family!"

"Oh, my God, Owen." Without thinking, Alex pulled him into a hug. "You should have told me."

Owen pushed Alex away. "Told you? Did you forget what you said to me when you found out I was married to Terry?!"

"What did you expect?" Alex bristled. "Not only did I find out my favorite uncle died, but he was secretly married to my best friend? The best friend I lost my virginity to!" Pent-up anger bubbled up in Alex. "Tell me, did it start when you moved in, or was it a gradual thing?"

Owen didn't realize he slapped Alex until after he had done it. "How fucking dare you?!" he growled, seething with anger. "While your mom and sister were off doing who knows what, and you were making your little sex videos, I was here taking care of Terry."

Owen was trembling with anger. Tears began rolling down his cheeks. "It's not like you told me you got engaged! I had to find out when your damn break up went viral on the Internet! To be honest, I expected you here sooner after that apparently tanked your career because everyone saw you for the asshole

you are. I'm surprised someone didn't hit you with their car sooner!"

"Fuck you." Alex snatched his bag off the couch, hiding the pain. "I'm going to bed."

Alex stormed down the hallway, slamming the bedroom door behind him. Tossing his bag into a corner, he stripped down to his designer white briefs. When he heard the door open, he turned to glare at Owen. Saying nothing, he climbed into the bed, lying on his side with his back to Owen.

"Well, it's good to know you started wearing underwear," Owen commented, climbing into bed.

Alex snarled, "What do you think you're doing?"

"It's my bed, asshole." Owen turned off the light. Resigned, he said, "Look, I'm sorry for what I said. It was below the belt. I'm tired and was trying to hurt you."

Alex asked, "What about slapping me?"

"I'm only sorry I didn't punch you instead," Owen answered with a slight chuckle.

Alex smiled. "Can we talk this out in the morning?"

"It is morning." Owen yawned. "We'll talk it out after my morning coffee."

Alex rolled over. Looking at the silhouette of his former friend, he felt a little more at ease. "Good night, Owen."

"Good night," Owen said sleepily. "Oh, and Alex, so we're clear, I don't care if your rooster crows in the morning. You're not going to cock a doodle do me."

# 4

# I'M READY

OWEN SIPPED HIS coffee. It was nearly noon and he still couldn't shake the exhaustion from lack of sleep. Alex was still sleeping in his bed. Waking up tangled with Alex, bodies pressed close and their roosters crowing at one another, he almost forgot all his problems. He almost forgot that Alex hated him, that he hated himself and Terry for hurting Alex with their secret.

Alex showing up at his front door was an unexpected welcomed complication. He knew he would have to confront Alex with the truth, eventually. He hoped eventually was going to be much, much later. There was no telling how Alex was going to react once he knew everything.

*He's going to hate me.* Owen poured himself another cup of coffee. *More than he already does.* Owen glanced longingly down the hall. *We spent every minute we could together that last summer. Kissing. Sucking. Holding each other.* Owen laughed to himself. *We thought Terry didn't know, but he knew. He made sure we had that last night together.*

*Owen lay on the couch, his head lying in Alex's lap. Sadness filled Alex's voice as he stroked Owen's hair. "I can't believe you're leaving in the morning."*

*"We have tonight," Owen commented, doing his best to hide the pain in his voice. That's all Owen would allow himself to have. Tonight. It was too much to hope that they would have more than that if Alex's mom had her way.*

*"I'll come and visit," Alex smiled down at him, "every chance I get."*

*Owen sat up. "I'd like that." He caressed Alex's cheek. With a shy smile, he said, "I'm ready."*

*"Really?" Alex's eyes grew big with excitement. "Are you messing with me? Because if you are..."*

*Owen cut him off with a kiss. "I'm sure."*

*"Oh, Owen," Alex moaned into the kiss. "Are you absolutely sure? I can wait."*

*Owen stood, pulling Alex up with him. "Absolutely sure."*

*"What about Uncle Terry?" Alex glanced at the door. "What if he comes home?"*

*Owen pulled Alex back to his room. "Let's not worry about him." He turned and wrapped his arms around Alex. "Tonight is about us and only us."*

*"I like that idea." Alex brushed his lips over Owen's. He ran a hand down Owen's side.*

*Owen let out a soft moan. "We have too many clothes on."*

Owen pulled up the hem of Alex's tank top. Pulling it up and off, he tossed it aside. He ran a hand over Alex's chest, feeling the developing hard muscles. He felt Alex shiver at his light touch, a mix of excitement and anticipation. He wanted this night to be special for Alex, a night he'd look fondly back on even if Alex ended up hating him.

Alex's breath hitched when Owen's fingertips brushed his over tiny rose-colored nipples. He leaned in, capturing Alex's mouth with his. Owen's hands glided over Alex's chest, then down his sides. Pushing his hands into Alex's gym shorts, he reached around to take hold of Alex's tight ass.

Deepening the kiss, Alex pulled him close. Owen moved from Alex's mouth to suck on the soft skin of Alex's neck. Tasting Alex on his tongue, he sucked on the soft skin, making Alex moan. Alex clawed at Owen's shirt. Owen dipped down lower, pausing to suckle Alex's nipple.

"Jesus! Fuck! Owen!" Alex cried out in pleasure, pulling Owen's shirt up. Owen paused long enough to let Alex pull his shirt off before latching onto the other nipple. Alex grabbed the back of Owen's head and let out a trembling low moan, "Oh, Owen."

Owen moved down, raining kisses over Alex's baby soft belly. Dropping to his knees, he pulled Alex's shorts down, allowing his hard cock to swing free. Owen looked up to see Alex smiling down at him with innocent desire. With a hand on Owen's shoulder, Alex stepped out of his shorts.

Needing his mouth to do something other than talk, Owen leaned forward and took Alex's balls into his mouth. He lavished each ball with careful strokes of his tongue. Alex stumbled back. Owen leaned forward with him, keeping the delicate orbs swaddled in his mouth.

"Damn," Alex groaned softly, falling back onto the bed. Leaning back, he ran a hand through Owen's hair and moaned, "Owen."

Owen pushed Alex's legs open. He moved to where Alex's thigh met his groin and teased the delicate spot. Alex gasped. Owen's mouth sucked and licked the sensitive skin, sending Alex's tense body thrashing about, barely able to catch his breath. Owen moved to right under his balls. He traced circles with his tongue, stimulating Alex but allowing him to catch his breath.

When Alex's breath calmed, Owen moved to the other side and sent Alex flailing about again. He knew all of Alex's spots and Alex knew his. They spent the better part of the summer secretly exploring one another's bodies, learning what they didn't like, what they liked, and, more importantly, what drove the other wild.

"You're going to pay for that," Alex panted, pushing Owen away. Owen lunged back, but Alex captured his mouth with his own. "My turn," he said wickedly.

Alex pulled Owen up to his feet, between his legs. He kissed Owen lightly over his chest and stomach, causing Owen to moan. Owen told Alex once that it was like fairies dancing over his skin when Alex did that. He undid Owen's shorts and let them fall to the floor, leaving Owen in just his white briefs.

Cupping Owen's butt, Alex pulled him closer. He wrote his name over and over again on Owen's flat belly with his tongue. Owen ran his hands through Alex's messy blond hair. Alex moved him back, dropping to his knees before Owen. Alex mouthed Owen's cock through the cotton briefs, massaging the hardness with his mouth.

*"Alex," Owen cried out softly, his nails scraping Alex's scalp. Alex began pulling down his briefs and freeing Owen's cock. They weren't even past his thighs before Alex had Owen's cock in his mouth. "Fuck, Alex," he moaned.*

*Alex moved his mouth along Owen's length with a familiar ease, savoring the taste of Owen in his mouth. Gripping Owen's ass, Alex rocked him back and forth, pushing and pulling Owen into his mouth. Owen, in turn, pulled Alex back and forth along his cock, pushing at the back of Alex's throat.*

*"Alex, you're too good at that," Owen warned, his voice trembling with the tingling in his balls.*

*Alex pulled off and stood. "Oh, no you don't." Taking Owen in his arms, he spun them around and pushed Owen onto the bed. He pulled Owen's underwear off and tossed them over his shoulders. Alex growled, "Keep your hands off your dick."*

*"What?" Owen laughed, inching his way back onto the bed.*

*Alex took hold of Owen's ankles and flipped him over. "You know it takes you forever to recover, and there are things I want to do before you leave." He smacked Owen on the ass. "Up on all fours."*

*"Say, please," Owen teased, then yelled, "Ouch," when Alex smacked him on the butt again. Getting up on all fours, he said, "Lube is in the nightstand."*

*Alex spread Owen's cheeks. "Good to know." He messaged the plump, youthful cheeks. "For later."*

*"What do you mean—?" Owen jumped and his eyes went wide when he felt Alex's tongue lick along his crack. Grinning, he relaxed and moaned, "Someone has been doing some research."*

*Fingers digging into Owen's skin, Alex's tongue danced and darted over Owen's hole. Driven by Owen's moans, Alex tried to spread him wider as he pressed his face farther into Owen. Alex's tongue dashed about, moving up and down in circles, zigzags, and scribbles over Owen's skin.*

*"Alex, oh, God, Alex." Owen fisted the sheets. He moved a hand underneath him, but Alex swatted his hand away with a growl. Owen tried again, but Alex stopped him again and again. "Alex, I need to cum!" Owen pleaded.*

*Alex swatted his hand away again. "Not until I tell you." Alex climbed up behind Owen. Rubbing the head of his cock up and down Owen's crack. "Unless you don't want me to fuck you."*

*"Ugh!" Owen moved his hand away from his dick. "Then fuck me already!"*

*Alex grabbed the lube from the nightstand. Popping the top, he drizzled lube down Owen's crack. The coldness caused him to jump. Alex rubbed the lube around Owen's hole before cautiously pushing a finger in.*

*"Did you, um, you know?" Alex asked cryptically, pushing a second finger in.*

*Owen glared back at him. "Yes. Do you think I would have said I was ready if I wasn't? Do I need to remind you of Terry's sex talks?"*

*"Not if you don't want me to go limp." Alex wiggled his fingers in Owen and was rewarded with a guttural groan. "Like that?"*

*Owen rolled his back. "Fuck yes."*

*"What about this?" Alex pushed a third finger into Owen, then ran them over the special spot in him. Owen shuddered. Alex chuckled. "Or this?" He did it again. Owen pounded the bed. "Or this?" He did it one more time.*

*Voice trembling, Owen cried out in need. "Alex!"*

*"We're revisiting this," Alex growled mischievously. He pulled his fingers from Owen, then lined his cock up. "Breathe."*

*Owen snapped, "I paid attention during the—" Owen gasped at the stretch of Alex's cock pushing into him. "Holy fuck!" He started taking in deep breaths and slowly letting them out.*

*"Are you okay?" Alex asked, leaving the head of his cock in Owen. "Do you need me to?"*

*Owen snapped, "Take it out." Closing his eyes, Owen took several deep breaths. "For just a minute."*

*"Okay." Alex pulled out. He ran a hand across Owen's back. "You tell me when."*

*After a few moments, Owen's breathing steadied. "Okay, go on."*

*"Relax." Alex pushed in, a little easier this time. Owen welcomed him in. "Are you okay?"*

*Owen nodded. "Go slow."*

*Fighting the urge to slam into Owen, Alex pushed in gingerly. He watched Owen for any sign of discomfort. "How does it feel?"*

*"It hurt at first, but now it feels so good." Owen rolled his neck, then his hips. "It feels real good."*

*Alex held onto Owen's hips. He rubbed his thumbs over the small of Owen's back. "I'm almost all the way in." His hips pressed into Owen. "I'm in. Are you okay?"*

*"If you ask me that one more time, I'm going to clench and rip your dick off," Owen growled. "Now fuck me already!"*

*Alex smacked Owen's ass. "Manners." He laughed at the glare Owen shot him over his shoulder. "Fine, I'll*

stop." He pulled out slightly then slid back in. "Oh, you're so tight."

Alex moved in and out of Owen, trying his best not to blow his load from the warm tightness that surrounded his dick. He felt Owen relax. Owen started bouncing back against him. Together, they picked up speed. Owen moaned, and Alex grunted. They fell into a rhythm.

Alex tightened his grip on Owen's hips. "I can't hold back." Alex reached up and grabbed Owen's shoulder. "Fuck! Owen!"

Owen reached under himself when Alex cried out. A few pumps, and his orgasmic scream joined Alex's. He gritted his teeth and rose up on his knees. Alex wrapped his arms around Owen, keeping Owen pressed close to his chest while he continued to thrust into Owen.

Stretching his neck, Owen turned his head to kiss Alex. Together they fell onto their sides, with Alex still nestled in Owen. Holding on tightly to Owen, Alex kissed the back of Owen's neck. Owen ran his fingers with a feather-like touch up and down Alex's arms.

"I love you, Owen," Alex whispered sweetly.

Owen hesitated for a moment. "I love you too, Alex."

"This asshole again." Owen rolled his eyes at the sight of Stewie's police cruiser coming down the drive. Setting his coffee down, he went to the front door. "I wonder what bogus charge he has for me today."

Opening the door, he stepped out onto the front porch. He watched Stewie get out of his car with his

mirrored sunglasses and put on his hat. The smile on Stewie's face sent a chill down Owen's spine. He walked up to Owen with a confident swagger, stopping at the base of the front porch.

"What do you want, Stewie?" Owen asked with an annoyed huff.

Cockily, Stewie grinned. "That's Officer Stuart Jackson."

"What do you want?" Owen rolled his eyes, ignoring the correction.

"That car over there was reported stolen." Stewie motioned to what Owen assumed was Alex's car. "I'm afraid I'm going to have to bring you in for questioning."

Owen scoffed. "Get real. You're not taking me anywhere. That car isn't stolen."

"Are you resisting arrest?" Stewie smiled eagerly. "Please, tell me you're resisting arrest."

# ENCOUNTERS IN UNDERWEAR

**A**LEX STIRRED IN the unfamiliar bed. Yawning and stretching, he reluctantly left the bed to ease his morning bladder pain. Scratching himself, he headed toward the main bathroom. Relieving himself, he glanced around. With sleep fading away as his bladder emptied, it hit him.

*This was Uncle Terry's bathroom.* He glanced back into the bedroom. *Was that Uncle Terry's bed?* He swallowed hard, a painful knot twisted in his stomach. *Did they share that bed?*

He shook off the last drops, then tucked his dick back into his black boxer briefs.

Stepping back into the bedroom, he ran his hand over the dresser. *He had his cologne bottles on display here.* When he looked at the top of the chest of drawers, he couldn't help but smile when he saw the picture of his Uncle Terry with his arms around Owen and him.

Stepping out into the hallway, he caught a glimpse of Owen going out the front door. Curious, he followed. Peeking out the window, he saw a police cruiser. He thought he recognized the man that got out of the cruiser. He couldn't believe it when Owen said his name.

*That bully is a cop?* Alex eavesdropped.

Old instincts kicked in. He spent most of his childhood being bullied by Stewie. When Owen arrived, he not only gained a friend, but an ally. He would have thought everyone left that bullshit in high school. Obviously, Stewie hadn't and was taking advantage of Owen being alone.

*Time to put an end to this.* Clad only in his boxer briefs, Alex opened the front door right as Stewie was taking a step onto the porch.

When Stewie saw him, he took a step back. Putting an arm over Owen's shoulder, Alex deepened his voice and asked, "Is there a problem here, Officer Stewie?"

"Officer Stuart Jackson," Stewie corrected with a sneer. "What kind of debauchery do you got going on in that house?"

Before Owen could say anything, Alex answered flippantly, "None of your business." He kissed Owen on the cheek. "Now, if you'll kindly get off our property," he glared at Stewie and put as much spite in his voice as he could when he said, "Stewie."

Bristling, Stewie corrected, "Officer Stuart Jackson." He looked Alex up and down. "I don't know what this sick deviant told you, but he doesn't really own this place."

Pursing his lips, Alex looked at Owen, then at Stewie. "True. The property is in his and my name. Alex Sparks." Alex grinned when he saw Stewie tense.

"Oh, and that car you claim was reported stolen is mine from the rental agency. I have the paperwork in the glove compartment if you'd like to see it." Alex took his arm from around Owen to cross his chest. "I have a feeling you don't, because you don't want to embarrass yourself like that."

"Does your mother know you're here?" Stewie's question shot through Alex.

Owen jumped in, his voice full of bitterness and anger. "I'm sure you'll notify her as soon as you're," Owen emphasized his next words, "off our property."

"I'll be back," Stewie said through gritted teeth. "With reinforcements."

Waving, Owen cheerfully called after Stewie, "Remember Danielle and Krystal aren't allowed on the property!"

"Really?" Alex asked loud enough for Owen to hear while fake smiling at Stewie stomping away.

When Stewie got into his police cruiser, Owen relaxed. "Yes." Watching Stewie pull away, he added, "There's a lot you don't know." He looked at Alex. "Come inside before he comes back and cites you for indecent exposure."

"I'm wearing underwear," Alex said, looking down at himself.

Stepping into the house, Owen chuckled, "Have you seen yourself in just your underwear?"

"Why aren't my mom and sister allowed on the property?" Alex followed Owen into the house.

Pouring himself a fresh cup of coffee, Owen asked, "Coffee?"

"Splash of milk, two sugars," Alex answered. "Are you going to tell me what's going on?"

Handing Alex his coffee, Owen asked, "Are you going to tell me what's going on with you?"

"Long story short, I figured if I was going to recover from being hit by a car after alienating everyone I know, I might as well do it in some place I own instead of my ex-fiancé's aunt's house." Alex sipped his coffee. "Good coffee."

Owen shrugged. "Sounds like it might be a good story." Moving over to the couch, he motioned for Alex to join him. "Want to tell me the long story?"

"What I want is to know what's going on around here." Alex joined him on the couch. "Why are my mom and sister not allowed on the property? Why is Stewie harassing you?" Alex looked down into his coffee. The hurt was evident in his voice. "Why didn't you tell me?"

Owen let out a heavy sigh. "Right for the jugular." Closing his eyes, he said, "Fuck. Terry, why did you have to die?" He looked at Alex with grave seriousness. "What I'm about to tell you, you're not going to want to hear. I promise you that it's the truth. Are you ready for it?"

"I need to know," Alex answered with a sigh.

Owen sat his coffee down. "You do, but I asked if you're ready."

"As ready as I'll ever be," Alex said, nervousness twisting his stomach. "Owen, tell me how you could sleep with me when you were married to my uncle? Did he know?"

Owen let out a humorless laugh. "Did you know he knew we were fooling around? He told me he was just relieved we waited until we were eighteen. He purposely stayed away that night so we could be together."

"Owen, you're evading the question," Alex accused, feeling the knife of that memory gut him.

Owen looked at him with a sad smile. "I married Terry for love. But not his, for yours. That's why I couldn't tell you."

"You're not making any sense," Alex said, shaking his head. "Why would you marry my Uncle Terry because you loved me? Why not marry me?"

Owen picked up his coffee and took a sip. Looking at Alex, he said with restrained anger, "I think it's time you learned what kind of people your mother and sister are." Owen bit his bottom lip. "Your mother was extorting money from Terry for years."

"I'm not listening to this." Alex stood up angrily. "You're a fucking liar."

Looking up at Alex, Owen said calmly, "I can show you the canceled checks or the video he recorded of her on the front porch confessing it all." Owen shrugged. "She didn't want a paper trail, but Terry made sure there was one and then he made sure he covered his ass for when he cut her off."

"My mother?" Alex sat down in disbelief. "What could she possibly use to blackmail Uncle Terry?"

Reaching out to take Alex's hand, Owen somberly said, "Us."

32

Puzzled, Alex looked at him, then his face turned to one of horror when it hit him. "Uncle Terry would never!"

"Doesn't matter, he would have been crucified once word got out. You wouldn't have been able to see him and I." Owen swallowed hard. "Well, I would have been gone."

Hearing the falter in Owen's voice, Alex asked quietly, "There's more to the story than you're letting on, isn't there?"

Downing the last of his coffee, Owen stood. "I'm going to get a fresh cup. Would you like one?" He took Alex's cup before he could answer. "You should put on a shirt or something."

"Okay." Alex stood. He caught Owen by the arm before he could leave. "I only want the truth."

# FAMILY SECRETS

**O**WEN USED THE few moments alone to gather himself. *Terry, you asshole. You promised me you'd be the one to tell him.* Owen set the two steaming cups on the table. He glanced over at Terry's picture. *Okay, you're not an asshole. You did save my life.*

"Okay, I'm ready." Alex sat down, dressed in a tank top and sweatpants. "Tell me everything."

Owen looked forward, keeping his eyes locked on the picture of Terry. "I'm not going to look at you while I tell you this." Owen swallowed hard. "You can look at me, but I'm not going to look at you." Owen took in a deep breath and let it out. "Okay?"

"Okay." Alex wanted to reach out to Owen, but instead, he interlaced his fingers in front of him.

Owen grew rigid. "I think it's time I told you why I moved in with Terry." Owen took in a deep breath and let it out slowly. "My father was ten years sober when he started drinking again. I don't know why. I hoped he'd get it together and sober up, but he didn't."

A tear ran down Owen's cheek. "We didn't have any other family I could turn to, so I called his sponsor, Terry." Owen's voice trembled. "He tried, but my dad didn't want to get sober. My dad knew if I stayed there, I'd end up in foster care, so he convinced Terry to take temporary custody of me." Owen kept his focus on Terry's picture. "My dad said that if Terry had me, he'd know where I was and that I was safe."

Owen wiped a stray tear. "The deal was, I'd come stay with Terry until my dad got sober and his life back together. My dad was supposed to check in twice a day, go to meetings, call Terry when he needed to, and meet him twice a week."

Alex shifted uncomfortably. "That's—"

"Don't speak." Owen cut him off. He exhaled loudly. "That's when I moved in here and met you." Owen closed his eyes. "My dad did what he was supposed to do for three weeks." Owen opened his eyes. They were filled with years of unshed tears. "Terry was ready to take me back to him, but my dad stopped calling. He wasn't answering his phone."

Owen's voice cracked with long-held pain. "My dad was doing so well and then he relapsed." Closing his eyes, Owen shook his head. "Terry found him, took him home, cleaned him up, and let my dad sleep it off. My dad started the program again. Then he relapsed again." Owen paused. "Terry was there to pick up the pieces every time he relapsed."

Owen wiped away the tears. Taking a deep breath, he continued, "Terry bought my dad a place to stay. Terry got my dad into an out-patient rehab." Owen exhaled loudly. Tears ran down his cheeks. "My dad

35

couldn't stay sober no matter how hard he tried. He stopped going to rehab and disappeared."

"Don't." Owen jerked away from Alex's touch. "That's why Terry was going to Springfield so much when I first got here. While he was there, he started buying up these properties, fixing them up, and renting them out or selling them."

Owen paused to collect himself. "He eventually started his own small company and hired a team to take care of the properties. This place is actually owned by that company, which really pissed your mom and sister off." Owen finally looked at Alex with red, watery eyes. "Are you ready to hear about your family?"

Alex didn't speak; only nodded. "You do realize that Terry didn't have a great childhood, right? Your grandmother treated him like trash, like your mother treats you." Owen held up a hand to keep Alex from speaking. "You know it's true. Everything is done for your sister and nothing for you."

Owen watched Alex recoil. "It was the same way for Terry. That's why he enlisted. To get away from them. He saw a lot of action. Turned to alcohol. Almost got kicked out. Got sober. Got out. Bought this land and built this house on it." Owen shook his head in disgust. "The only time Terry heard from your grandma and mom was when they needed money."

"They tried to force their way into this house and force Terry out." Owen looked at Alex coldly. "They were evicted from so many places that no one would rent to them, so Terry put them up in a house in town." Owen rolled his eyes. "Your mother didn't even invite Terry to her wedding. He found out second hand that

36

your grandmother died, and when she gave birth to Krystal and to you."

Owen focused back on the picture of Terry. "After your father mysteriously died, your mother used you and Krystal to guilt money out of Terry. When your sister got married…" Owen looked at Alex with hurt and anger in his eyes. "Terry paid for your sister's weddings. Both of them. Your mother threatened to never let Terry see you ever again if he didn't."

"I… I didn't know." Alex's voice was filled with hurt and shame.

Owen looked back at Terry's photo on the wall. "Terry had enough of your mother and your sister using him as a bank, and he cut them off. He threatened to take custody of you, among other things." Owen let out a humorless laugh. "Then I moved in and your mother struck. She sank her teeth back into Terry."

Owen took a deep breath. "I saw it firsthand when you weren't here. The fights he had with her. The demands they made. The threats about us." Owen motioned to the door. "That's when he got those cameras installed. She didn't know they were there when he baited her into a fight where she confessed everything."

Owen wrapped his arms around himself. "The things she said to Terry. I heard her. I was right behind the door listening." He looked at Alex. "I didn't know what she meant at the time, but she told Terry that she'd hate for him to end up like her husband or Krystal's first husband."

"That doesn't make any sense." Alex looked at Owen, confused. "My father died when I was six. They told me he had a heart attack and Krystal's husband died in a car accident." Alex paused. "When did Krystal get remarried? And to whom?"

Owen scoffed. "We just kicked him off the property."

"Oh, shit," Alex gasped.

Owen nodded. "Terry was scared of what your mom and sister would do. He did some digging. Your mother took out a huge life insurance policy a few months before your dad died. Krystal did the same for her husband." He looked at Alex. He needed Alex to believe him. "Terry started digging, and it fucking scared him. Your father didn't die of a heart attack. They listed it as the cause of death, but Terry found out that your dad also had a broken neck and several broken ribs. Krystal's husband's car was leaking brake fluid right after his tune-up."

When Alex looked at him, confused, Owen clarified, "They lied about his cause of death so your mother could collect his life insurance." At Alex's eyebrow raise, Owen blurted out, "Alex! Your mother and sister killed their husbands for the money!"

"No." Alex jumped up, shaking his head. "You're lying. My mother loved him!" Hurt and pain crossed Alex's face as the realization hit him. His voice dropped low. "My mother loved him. She'd never hurt him."

Owen swallowed hard. "When did she take the policy out on you?"

"Six months ago. She told me it was…" Alex's voice was barely a whisper. His body trembled. "I need to get out of here."

"The hit and run." A chill ran down Owen's spine. He knew the answer but still asked, "Who is the beneficiary?"

"I… I…" Alex fisted his hair with both hands. "I need to get out of here."

Owen stood. Reaching out to console Alex, he asked, "It's your mother, isn't it?"

Alex pulled away from Owen's touch. He opened his mouth to say something, but instead ran to the front door.

# THE TRUTH HURTS

**A**LEX BURST OUT the front door and hurled himself off the porch onto the soft grass, landing on all fours, eyes stinging from the tears. A moment later, the contents of his stomach were splattered on the ground below him. His stomach continued to convulse as if it were trying to turn itself inside out.

*Has anyone in my life ever really loved me?* Spittle and snot dripped from his chin as Alex craned his head to the sky and shouted, "Has anyone in my life ever really loved me?!" Lowering his head, eyes stinging with tears, breathing heavily, and throat burning from emptying his stomach, Alex asked softly, "Does anyone even care about me?!"

"I care about you," Owen answered quietly. Kneeling down, he rubbed Alex's back. "I know you don't think so, but I always cared about you."

Alex refused to turn his head and look at Owen. "Yeah, you cared about me enough to fuck me before marrying my uncle the next day." Alex wiped his mouth, then sat up. "You cared about me enough to disappear when you went to school." Alex pushed himself to his feet. He glared at Owen, hands bunching up into fists. "You cared about me enough to wait for me to find out when my uncle died that you were secretly married to him."

Standing up and brushing off his knees, Owen stiffened. "I cared about you enough not to hurt you." Owen motioned back to the house. "Want to get cleaned up and I can tell you the rest?" All of Owen's compassion turned to anger. "Fine. Stay out here and throw a tantrum. You'll have to come inside, eventually." Owen started for the house. "All your shit's in here, remember?"

"Asshole." Alex stomped after Owen.

He went straight to the hall bathroom. Turning on the faucet, he splashed water on his face, then cupped water in his hands to wash the acrid taste from his mouth. Spitting into the sink, he grabbed a hand towel and dried his face. Chest heaving with anger, he glowered at his reflection.

*Everyone I ever thought loved me never did.* Alex fisted the towel in his hand. *No wonder I became a cold-hearted bitch.* He fought the urge to slam his fist into the mirror. *I need answers.*

Alex stormed back into the living room. Owen sat calmly and collected on the sofa. On the coffee table sat two fresh cups of coffee. Saying nothing, Alex returned to his spot on the sofa. Owen still said nothing. Alex picked up the coffee but hesitated when he brought it to his lips.

"It's not poisoned," Owen said with a humorless laugh.

Alex took a healthy sip, then set the coffee down. "I need answers." He kept his eyes locked on Owen. "I want you to look me in the eyes and tell me the truth about everything."

"Okay." Owen glanced at the photo of Terry, then back at Alex. "You and Terry had similar childhoods. He was the younger brother that was neglected and turned into a servant by his mother." Owen looked intently at Alex. "Just like you." He held up a hand to keep Alex from speaking. "Terry enlisted the moment he could and wasn't planning on looking back, but your grandmother had a hold on him, just like your mother has a hold on you."

Owen motioned to the house. "Terry did well for himself once he got sober. Made some good investments. Saved up a whole lot of money. Good thing since your grandmother didn't leave him anything in her will." Owen guffawed. "Your family only cared about what Terry could do for them, not him. I can't believe the shit he put up with."

"Owen…" Alex's voice grew somber. "I didn't know."

Picking up his coffee, Owen said, "I know." He took a sip. "The money from your father's life insurance lasted her a while, then she needed Terry's help. He was her personal bank. When he cut her off is when she made the threat. That's when Terry came up with the plan."

Owen looked at Alex with imploring eyes. "I didn't know about the plan until after graduation. I swear." Setting the coffee down, he looked at Terry's

picture. "You stupid, wonderful jerk." He looked back at Alex. "Terry was buying up properties, renovating them, and renting them out. He was making a lot of money and was scared your mom would try to take it from us when he passed. That's why he started a company. He wanted to protect his assets from her. This property is in the company's name."

"Wait," Alex said, confused. "I thought this place was in both of our names."

Angrier than he intended, Owen said, "If you had stuck around long enough to find out, you would have learned that he didn't leave us shit. We already owned it. If you hadn't stormed out of town after the funeral or answered one of my calls, you would have known that." Owen closed his eyes. "I'm sorry. I know you were angry and hurt by everything."

Owen wrapped his arms around himself. "Terry was sick. That's the other reason he went to town so often. He hid it from us, but your mother knew. She knew, and she was hovering like a vulture waiting to pick away at his carcass." Owen shot Alex a look, telling him to keep quiet. "Terry needed someone he could trust to be in charge of his medical care and finances that your mother couldn't intimidate."

Owen reached out and took Alex's hand. "Your mother has the whole town convinced she is this pious, wronged woman and bends everyone to her will. We never meant to hurt you in the process. That was the last thing either of us ever wanted, but your mother is cruel and merciless. Terry figured the only way to keep her from strong-arming me out was to make me his husband."

"How long?" Alex asked, his voice filled with hurt and pain. "How long were you two…?" Alex couldn't finish the question.

Giving Alex's hand a squeeze, Owen answered, "Terry and me never had a sexual relationship. It was solely business." He shot the picture of Terry a dirty look. "You slick bastard." He turned back to Alex. "When Terry proposed his plan, it made sense at the time. After going through everything, it still makes sense now."

Owen took his hand back. "Terry and I got married so I would have his medical coverage from his military service and to make it impossible for your mother to try to take control of his medical treatment when he got sick." Owen swallowed hard. "She tried, oh, she tried. She even tried to have our marriage contested to try and gain control."

Owen shook his head at Alex's confused look. "Yeah, your mother knew about my marriage to Terry long before his death, no matter what she says."

"Why didn't you or Terry tell me what was going on?" Alex asked, unsure what part to be hurt by.

Owen looked at Alex incredulously. "When you were here, you were under your mother's thumb. We were scared you'd tell her and ruin everything Terry was setting in motion. Then you disappeared. Terry was delayed a few weeks because he got sick from a treatment. When he came back, he couldn't find you. Your phone stopped working, and we didn't know how to contact you. Trust me. I tried. I even contacted your agent."

"Ex-agent. He was useless." Alex sighed. "You're right. She used to grill me about Terry after every visit. I didn't think about it at the time. She was probably trying to get dirt out of me." He shook his head. "I disappeared because I thought you two abandoned me like my mother and Krystal did." He swallowed hard. "I came back so many times to this place, hoping to see you here waiting for me."

Owen reached out and touched Alex's knee. "I'm so sorry." He focused back on Terry's picture. "Your mother is why Terry forbade us from doing anything. He didn't want us used against him or me taken from him."

Alex shifted uncomfortably on the couch. "Why is Stewie harassing you?"

Picking up his coffee, Owen took a long sip before answering. "Terry's money and property. After we got married, Terry started transferring all his assets into my name: bank accounts, stocks, bonds." Owen smiled triumphantly. "The first thing he did was change the beneficiary of his life insurance from your mom to me."

Owen looked around. "Everything went into my name except this place. That he put in the company's name. The company he put both our names on." He glanced over at Terry's picture. "He said he wanted to make sure we always had a place to come back to, so we'd always find each other again." Owen took a second before admitting, "Really, the only reason I'm still here was the off chance you'd come back here like Terry thought you would."

Turning back to Alex, he said, "When your mother found out Terry had no assets and he had switched

the beneficiary on the life insurance, she started a war against me and enlisted your sister."

"What did they do?" Alex felt guilty for not being there for Owen, for Terry.

Owen exhaled angrily. "They turned the entire town against me. They went online to spread all these lies about me, telling people I'm a gold digger, that Terry and I had an inappropriate relationship, that I run some drug empire out of here." Owen trembled with anger. "The police started harassing me every time I went into town, then started coming out here for stupid shit. That's why I had to get a lawyer. Thankfully, Terry had those cameras installed."

"Why though?" Alex asked, trying to make sense of it all. "What did they think would come from it?"

Owen's voice cracked when he spoke. "Crowdfunding and donations. Since they couldn't get any money out of Terry or me, they've been bilking the public, saying they need help with legal fees to fight me." Owen began to tremble. "I barely can get any sleep. I have to be on guard every time I leave here. I can't go anywhere at night."

"I'm so sorry." Alex reached over and pulled Owen into his arms. "I wish I had been here for you."

Owen relaxed into his arms. "You were going through your own shit."

"What about school?" Alex asked quietly. "Did you ever finish?"

Owen let himself feel comfort in Alex's embrace. He'd been fighting for so long on his own that he forgot what it was to feel safe. "I did, but Terry started getting sick during my last year. I didn't get to walk

46

or do any internships. I was at his side every moment I could be."

"At least someone who loved him was there." Alex couldn't help the guilt he felt for not keeping in touch with his Uncle Terry. "I really should have done better, been better to him and everyone else in my life."

Owen ran a finger along Alex's biceps. "It's not too late to make things right with people."

"It's not too late for you to start your journalism career." Alex pulled Owen closer. He relaxed, no longer sure where to direct his anger.

Owen's body shook with a sarcastic chuckle. "I live in a town where everyone hates me. Who knows what your bitch mom and sister would do if I left this property." Owen turned to look at Alex. "I was gone for a weekend and came back to your mom showing the land to a potential buyer."

Owen turned and laid his head on Alex's chest. "How can I start my career in journalism? I can't go out and look for news to report on because in this town I'm always the news. If I leave the area, I'll come back to a huge legal battle to get my home back." Owen couldn't hide the despair in his voice. "She's turned me into a prisoner in my home." He glared at Alex. "A home I don't even want anymore."

"I'm here now." Alex looked at Terry's picture. "Like when we were younger, it's me and you against the world." He kissed the top of Alex's head. "We'll get through this together."

Owen pulled himself away from Alex. Seeing the sadness on Alex's face, he asked, "Why are you

here? Why did you come back? No bullshit. Tell me everything."

"That's a story." Alex thought for a moment as an idea hit him. "How would you like to tell it?"

# 8

# SMILE! YOU'RE ON CAMERA

**"N**o. Absolutely not." Owen stood and moved away from Alex. "I can't believe you would even suggest it."

Standing, Alex put a hand on Owen's shoulder. "Owen, it's a great idea. You can ask me whatever you want and I'll answer honestly. Give me one reason why it's not a good idea."

"How about I don't have any of the equipment needed for what you want," Owen answered, putting up a finger. Putting up a second finger, he said, "It'll never get seen. No one is going to air something done by a nobody like me." Owen put up a third finger. "I don't want to do it."

Alex put Owen's index finger down. "We'll get the equipment and I know how to edit the footage." He put down Owen's ring finger. "Yes, you do. I see it in your eyes." He kissed Owen's middle finger before putting it down. "You're not a nobody."

"I'll think about it." Owen poked Alex in the chest. "If I do this, you have to answer honestly. I'll know if you're lying."

Alex smiled. "Great." He winked at Owen. "When are we going to the police station?"

"What?" Owen looked at Alex, dumbstruck. "You're not going to the police station with me."

Alex darted his eyes back and forth. "You're not going by yourself after everything you told me. Plus, it'll be good to let people know I'm back in town." Alex winked at him. "I'm going to get ready."

Watching Alex head back to the room, Owen said to himself, "This is a bad idea."

Owen's nervous apprehension quickly turned into angry rage when the male officer at the front desk groaned with a roll of his eyes at the sight of him. "What did we supposedly do now?"

"There's no supposedly about it," Alex barked out before Owen could say anything. Standing in front of the desk with his shoulders thrust back and chest puffed out, he challenged the officer with his stare. "Why don't you go get your boss since you can't seem to take a complaint seriously?"

Unintimidated, the officer slapped two pieces of paper onto a clipboard and thrust it toward Owen. "Police Chief Anders doesn't handle frivolous complaints."

"Do you mind repeating that," Alex pulled out his phone and aimed the camera at the officer, "for my 1.2 million followers?"

"You can't record in here!" the officer shouted, jumping up from his desk and trying to snatch Alex's phone.

Evading the officer, Alex spoke loud enough for everyone in the station to hear. "I certainly can. You're in a public building." Seeing the two other on-duty officers getting up from their desks, Alex said, "Go ahead and give your name to my," he emphasized his next words, "my 1.4 million followers."

"Alex," Owen nervously warned, "you're causing a scene."

Red-faced, the front desk officer put his hand on his stun gun. "I'm giving you one last chance to stop recording before I arrest you!"

"Try it," Alex challenged, "and see how fast I have this police station under a national microscope."

"Stand down, Officer Mason," a gruff, country-accented voice calmly ordered. A portly gray-haired officer with a handlebar mustache came out of the back office. Coming up to the front desk officer, he put a hand on the angry officer's shoulder. "Why don't you go take a break?" To Alex and Owen, he asked, "Can I help you fellas? I'm Police Chief Anders."

Skulking away, the desk officer muttered under his breath, "Fucking fags."

"What was that?" Alex asked loudly, holding his phone up. "My 1.6 million followers didn't catch that."

Police Chief Anders moved to block the camera with his body. "I'd be glad to help you, but first you need to stop recording."

"Nope." Alex moved so he had Anders's face centered in the camera. "Jackson vs. the City of Lickmaold. Federal court ruled civilians can record police officers in all aspects of their duties unless sensitive information may be viewed." Alex winked at Anders with a smug grin. "I called my attorney on the way here."

Anders let out a dramatic sigh. "Fine. What can I help you boys with?"

"Owen." Alex motioned for him to speak.

It took Owen a moment to realize everyone, including Alex's followers, was waiting for him to speak. "Um, yes, your Officer Stewie came by place in the middle of the night on a false noise complaint and again this morning claiming his," he motioned to Alex, "rental car was stolen. Both times, he threatened me with an illegal arrest and falsely claimed the property was not mine."

"I'll take care of it." Anders looked from Owen to Alex, then back to Owen. "Is that what all these theatrics were for?"

Something in Owen snapped. He wasn't sure if he'd had enough or if it was Alex being there, but all his pent-up anger erupted with Alex getting it all on camera. "Theatrics?! How many times have I come in and lodged similar complaints over the past three years?! And what have you done?! Nothing!"

"I suggest you watch your tone, boy," Anders warned. "There's not much I can do since you're not the rightful owner of that property."

Shocked, Alex spoke up. "Excuse me? All the paperwork lists him as one of the owners."

"I don't give a damn what some paper says," Anders said, anger seeping into his voice. "Everyone in this town knows that land should have gone to Terry's rightful family, not this parasite."

Putting a hand up to stop Owen from responding and keeping his phone trained on Police Chief Anders, Alex said coolly, "I'd appreciate it if you didn't call my uncle a parasite." They watched realization slowly don on Anders's face. "Yeah, also, my attorney will be subpoenaing all the dispatch logs and calls concerning our property." Alex put an arm around Owen. "I suggest you start getting your shit together and leave us alone."

"Have a nice day," Owen said with a triumphant smile and a wave before Alex maneuvered him out.

Once they were outside, Alex let go of Owen. Turning off his phone and returning it to his pocket, they both burst out into laughter. "Did you see that vein in his forehead throb when he realized who I was?"

"You weren't really broadcasting live? Were you?" Owen asked, laughing as he moved to the passenger side of Alex's rental.

Getting into the driver's seat, Alex grinned. "No, I closed all my social media accounts, but I was recording."

"That's why your follower count kept changing!" Owen howled with laughter. "The lawyer and court case were fake too, weren't they?"

Starting up the car and carefully backing out of the parking space, Alex chuckled. "The city of lick my

53

ole? Fake?" Putting the car in drive and heading home, Alex grew serious. "The lawyer is fake for now. How has your attorney not put a stop to them?"

"I don't know." Owen looked at the notification on his phone. "Fuck."

Concerned, Alex asked, "What now?"

"Your mother is at the house." Owen typed furiously into the phone. "I'm calling in a favor."

# 9

# FAMILY REUNION

**A**LEX'S STOMACH TWISTED with anger and dread the closer they got to their home. He was conflicted about seeing his mother and sister. The last time he spoke to his mother was a few days after his breakup with Cameron. She had asked for—no, demanded—money. She wouldn't get off the phone until he sent it, and cut him off when he tried to tell her about the breakup.

He couldn't remember the last time he'd spoken to his sister. He'd reached out to both his sister and his mother after he'd woken up in the hospital room to the steady sounds of beeping machines and harsh fluorescent lighting to see his ex, Cameron, sitting there with his new boyfriend Carlos.

He lost count of how many unanswered texts and calls sent to voicemail there were before Lexi took the phone from him and urged him to rest. He saw the quiet pain in her face for him. She knew. She knew and said nothing. Instead, she swaddled Alex in her protective love like the mother his should have been.

Alex looked at his mother through the car windshield with her overly dyed thinning ruddy brown hair, her blotchy pale face lined with wrinkles that made her look ten years older than her fifty-some years. Her angry, disapproving scowl made her plump, barely five-foot body seem much bigger and menacing.

Beside her stood his annoyed and disapproving sister, Krystal. Her long, frizzy, dull brown hair was pulled into a tight ponytail that pulled her already tight face tighter. She stood maybe an inch taller than their mother. Her curvy body was losing its shape as she was slowly turning into a knock off clone of their mother.

Getting out of the car, Alex wasn't sure what he was going to say to them. Before he could say a word, Owen was out of the car and slamming the door behind him. Alex looked at Owen trembling with seething anger, about to snap. He turned his attention to the subjects of Owen's anger standing on the front porch, glaring back at him.

Owen snarled, "What are you doing on my property? You know you're not allowed to be here." Through clenched teeth, Owen added, "Any of you."

"It's not your property, thief," Danielle tossed back at him, her voice dripping with hate and bitterness. She turned her venom toward Alex. "What are you doing with him?"

Alex wasn't sure what he was going to say until it came out of his mouth. "Like you really care." Alex felt a weight lift from his soul. "Now answer his question."

"How dare you talk to Mom like that?" Krystal hissed. "She and I deserve respect after all we've done for you, despite being the embarrassment you are."

The rose-colored glasses Alex saw his mother and sister through shattered. The lies and justifications he had told himself about them were washed away by a tsunami of anger and hurt. "Done for me?" He gave them both an incredulous look. "The only thing you've ever done for me is treat me like an indentured servant and bank."

Alex focused his words on his mother. "What you did was poison me against the people who loved me because you wouldn't." His eyes stung with years of unshed tears. "What you did was teach me that I was nothing to you unless you needed something from me."

"Since you were conceived you've done nothing but disappoint me!" Danielle meant the words to sting like a crack of a whip, but Alex felt nothing. "You owe me for bearing the shame of your filthy, sinful ways. Just like your Uncle Terry."

Owen's voice cut like lightning through the sky. "Keep his name out of your mouth."

"Why? Because you couldn't keep his dick out of yours?" Stewie chuffed. "Sick freaks."

Owen felt his anger boiling up in him. He had enough. "Get off our property." Putting force in his words, he added, "Now."

"It's not your property," Danielle hissed. "It's mine."

Feeling emboldened, Alex smirked. "The paperwork says differently." He pointed behind him to the road. "Now go, before I enforce the paperwork that says you can't be here."

"We'll see who is leaving." The amusement in Stewie's voice unsettled Alex.

Alex and Owen turned to see a police cruiser slowly moving down the road. The lights flashed with a short burst of its siren. Looking at Owen, who had a smug grin on his face, Alex was confused. The cruiser pulled up and parked alongside the passenger side of the car. The side Owen was on. Alex began to worry.

A tall, broad-shouldered young man with short, ruddy red hair and freckled, pale skin stepped out of the cruiser. He nodded at Stewie, then turned to Owen and said in a thick country accent, "I understand you have some trespassers you need to remove, Mr. Sparks."

"Officer Flynn, you know this land doesn't rightly belong to him!" Stewie bellowed from the porch. "Danielle is the rightful owner."

Turning his sapphire blue eyes to the front porch, there was no denying the satisfaction in his voice when he addressed Stewie. "I think you need to keep your mouth shut until you speak to Chief Anders." Officer Flynn's grin stretched across his chiseled, smooth face. "He's not too happy with you. As for those two ladies you're with, I know they aren't allowed on this property or within one hundred feet of Mr. Sparks here."

"I want them off the property now," Owen instructed.

Alex heard the slight hint of defeat in Owen's voice, and his heart went out to him. "No." Owen and Officer Flynn stood there in shock while Danielle,

Krystal, and Stewie smiled triumphantly. Alex then added, "I want them arrested. We're pressing charges."

"You can't do that!" Krystal shrieked. "Baby! Do something!"

Officer Flynn started moving to the porch. "Ladies, don't resist." He fixed his gaze on Stewie. "Don't you interfere. You're in enough hot water as it is."

"Honey, I can't do anything." Stewie stepped away from Danielle and Krystal. "I'll get you out, I promise."

Danielle stepped back, shrieking, "Don't you put your hands on me!"

"Stewie!" Krystal screamed as Officer Flynn took her by the arm and slapped a handcuff on her wrist, then spun her around to lock it with the other behind her back.

Danielle tried to evade Officer Flynn, but was trapped on the small porch. She shrieked as he quickly subdued her. "I'll have your badge for this!"

"You can try, ma'am." Officer Flynn guided her over to her daughter, who was screaming at her husband. "Now, if you two would be ever so kind as to exercise your rights to remain silent, I would be very much appreciative."

Owen moved to stand beside Alex. "You had your mother and sister arrested," he said in awe as Officer Flynn read them their rights and ushered them into the back of his cruiser. "Why?"

"Maybe I want to teach them a lesson." Alex put an arm over Owen's shoulder. "Maybe I'm tired of pushing away everyone who loves me and I think it's time to try and fix those broken relationships."

Officer Flynn tapped the top of Alex's rental. "I'll meet you boys at the station." He looked over at a stunned Stewie. "I suggest you get your butt over to the station, too. Captain Anders has some words for you."

# CAMERON'S CALL

**A**LEX WAS QUIET. Lost in his thoughts after leaving the police station for a second time that day, he handed the car keys to Owen and wordlessly got into the passenger's side. Owen didn't pry. He didn't know what to say that would fix the broken man he once called a friend and had hoped to one day call his lover.

*I have to give him time and space,* Owen reasoned while navigating the drive back home. *He's had a lot thrown at him today.* Owen covertly glanced at Alex from the corner of his eyes. *He's still that frail young man I knew under that hard exterior. Maybe I should seriously consider telling his story.*

Owen took his hand off of the wheel to take Alex's. *We don't need to talk for him to know I'm here for him.* Owen smiled softly when Alex squeezed his hand. *Like he was there for me today.*

They let go of each other's hands after Owen parked. When they left the car, they gravitated to each other going up to the house, letting their fingers brush. Alex nearly had his chest pressed to Owen's back while he unlocked the door and deactivated the alarms.

"I need to take a shower," Alex announced after a long period of them standing in the living room in an uncomfortable silence.

Owen followed him to the room, unsure of the exact reason why other than he didn't want to leave Alex alone.

"Did you want to shower with me?" Alex asked, pulling off his shirt.

Owen grabbed for the first lie he could. "I was going to make the bed." He pulled the pillows off the bed. Alex's phone landed in the middle of the folds of the comforter.

"Can you put that on to charge for me?" Alex asked, dropping his pants.

Taking the phone off the bed, Owen looked up to see Alex standing there, completely naked. *He's so comfortable standing there naked in front of me.* His eyes lingered over Alex's toned body. *Is it because of what we were or because of his life in porn?*

"Sure." Alex's phone vibrated in Owen's hand. Glancing at the screen, he said, "Someone named Cameron sent you a text. Isn't he your ex?"

Alex's body tensed slightly. "I'll call him later."

"Okay." Owen set the phone on the wireless charger. He turned to see Alex walking into the bathroom. *Damn,* Owen mouthed in appreciation of Alex's strong, muscled back and toned ass. *He's definitely not the skinny boy I remember.*

Owen started tugging at the sheets and brushing out the wrinkles. He heard the shower turn on. *We're going to have to share a bed again tonight.* He pulled the comforter up. *Do I really mind?* He fluffed the pillows, then sat them in their spots. *Is this a second chance for us?*

The sound of Alex's phone ringing snapped him out of his thoughts. He looked at the screen and saw Cameron's name on it. He looked at the bathroom and heard the shower still running. He reached out for the phone, but it was too late. The call was sent to voicemail.

A second later, Cameron's name flashed on the screen. Owen didn't hesitate this time. He wasn't sure why he wanted to talk to Cameron, other than he probably had some answers to the real reasons Alex came home. Answering the call, he put the phone to his ear.

"Why have you been avoiding my calls and texts?!" Came Cameron's shrill voice. "And where the fuck are you?!"

Owen didn't think before he answered. "My bedroom."

"You're not Alex! What the Hell?!" There was a hint of fear in Cameron's voice. He then demanded, "Who are you and where is Alex?!"

Owen chose his words carefully. "Alex is in the shower. I'm Owen, an old high school friend."

"An old high school friend," Cameron said suspiciously.

Owen didn't have time for lengthy explanations. He didn't want Alex to catch him. "He showed up on my doorstep early this morning. A lot has happened

since then. I mean a lot." Owen glanced at the bath-room door. "Look, I'm not sure how he's going to react to me talking to you. Can I give you my number and you can text me yours and I'll call you once Alex isn't around?"

"You promise me he's okay," Cameron demanded.

Owen heard the water shut off. "If I could promise you that, I wouldn't be talking to you behind his back. Now, are you ready for my number?"

"Fine," Cameron said with annoyance.

Owen rattled his number off. A second later, a text came through on his phone from Cameron. "Got it. I'll text or call you as soon as I can." He quickly hung the phone up and put it back on the charger.

"You didn't have to wait for me," Alex commented, stepping out of the bathroom with a towel around his waist, and his hair and skin dripping with water. "Look, I know it's been a rough couple of hours. I just need some time to process it all, that's it."

Owen stumbled over his words. "I wasn't waiting for you."

"Then what were you doing?" Alex asked, pulling clothes out of his bag.

*Trying not to get caught,* Owen thought before spit-ting out the lie. "I was thinking of where we can put your clothes." At Alex's confused look, he explained, "You can't keep all your things in your bags. They'd get wrinkled and you'll never find your underwear."

Alex chuffed. "I can go without underwear."

"I also don't want to be tripping over your bags in the middle of the night," Owen scolded.

Alex pulled out a pair of red trunks from his duffle bag. "Once I move into the other room, you won't have to worry about it."

"About that..." Owen ran a nervous hand through his hair. "Maybe we could look into doing that inter-view thing you wanted." He saw a mixture of fear and hope on Alex's face. He shifted his weight from foot to foot. "When you're ready. We still have to get every-thing we need to do it and set the room up."

Alex's smile faltered. "Thanks." He looked down at the clothes in his hands. "I'm going to get dressed." He looked up at Owen, was about to say something, but headed to the bathroom instead.

*He has some demons.* Owen pulled out his phone and looked at the text from Cameron. *Maybe with a little help, I can help him. I owe him that much after what I put him through.*

"I think I might go for a walk around the prop-erty, to clear my head," Alex called from the bathroom. "Maybe walk some of the trails we used to when we were younger if they aren't grown over."

[OWEN: I'll call you in a little bit.] He sent to Cameron.

"The ones to and from town aren't," Owen called back, slipping the phone in his pocket. "I'm going to make some room for your stuff in here."

Alex stepped out wearing black sweatpants, a fash-ionably distressed tee, hair still slightly damp from his shower. "Do dirty old men still roam those trails?"

"You'll be the first in a while," Owen answered cheekily.

Smiling, Alex grumbled playfully, "Asshole," as he left.

Owen pulled open the one drawer in the dresser that held anything. He pulled the old fleece blanket out that he and Alex would snuggle under while watching movies on cold winter days. It was the very same blanket Terry wanted with him in the hospital because it was filled with love.

He brought the blanket up to his face and inhaled. *It still smells like his aftershave.* Owen's eyes stung with tears. *I never got to grieve over you.* He hugged the blanket to his chest, eventually setting it on the bed.

Wiping away the previously unshed tears, he went to sit out front on the porch. He pulled out his phone to look at the assigned contact number. He debated if it was a good idea to go behind Alex's back like this. He hit call.

Cameron answered on the first ring. "Owen?"

"Yeah." Owen hoped Cameron couldn't hear the tears in his voice. "He went for a walk in the woods, so we got some time."

Cameron's voice became accusatory. "Good, because I have some questions, like who the fuck you really are?"

"I'm Owen, a friend of his from high school," he hesitated a second, then added, "I was also his first boyfriend and," Owen swallowed hard, "his uncle's widower." Owen gave out a humorless laugh at the resounding silence. "Are you ready for a fucked up story?"

Cameron stayed silent while Owen recounted everything that had happened. He knew by the sounds Cameron made whether he was relieved, shocked, worried, or had more questions. After going through it all, Owen realized he had questions like how it hadn't barely been twelve hours with all this happening.

"Your turn," Owen announced when he was done. "What happened to bring Alex to my door?"

"Hold on," Cameron said, exasperated. "You think his mother might have been involved in the hit and run?"

Owen's stomach twisted. "Yes, given the suspicious family history."

"And he had her and his sister arrested today for trespassing?" Cameron chuckled softly.

Infected by Cameron's amusement, Owen laughed out, "Yeah."

"You married his uncle?" there was a devilish playfulness in Cameron's voice. "So Alex's first love, first kiss, and first time was with his uncle."

Owen growled to hide his amusement at the realization. "I wasn't his uncle then and I'm only his uncle by marriage, not blood."

"How very hillbilly chic," Cameron laughed. "Oh, I needed that laugh after spending the last week trying to get a hold of him."

Owen stopped laughing. "Wait. You haven't been able to get a hold of him for a week and he got here this morning. Where has he been?"

"Only he could tell us," Cameron answered, growing serious. "At least he's safe now."

Owen chewed on his lower lip. "You're right. Do you want to tell me what brought him to me?"

"I think it was a combination of things," Cameron answered with a sigh. "No one wanted to work with him because they thought my Aunt Lexi wouldn't cast them if they did. Honestly, she could have cared less. She knows how to separate work and personal. Studios were passing him up because of our viral breakup."

Cameron sighed. "I officially started dating Carlos. He had to move out of my condo." Sadness filled Cameron's voice. "We found out after that he was hotel hopping and crashing at people's places when he could. When he woke up in the hospital, he wasn't exactly happy to see me, Lexi, and Carlos there."

Cameron grimaced. "Carlos wasn't too happy to be there either, but that's another story. That's when we found out he didn't have any place to go and Aunt Lexi made the decision that he was coming home with her." Cameron chuckled. "He knew better than to argue."

Cameron's voice went solemn. "He tried contacting his mother, but she never answered, never called back, and didn't even text." Cameron added angrily, "What a bitch."

"You have no idea," Owen commented bitterly.

Cameron snorted. "Well, she's in jail for the time being." Cameron sighed. "I'm guessing he felt like he had no other place to go."

"To the person who hurt him the most," Owen lamented.

"Or to the person who loved him the most," Cameron suggested. "Are you serious about interviewing him?"

Owen answered without hesitation. "I am. Once we get all the equipment we need."

"Do you know what you are doing?" Cameron asked. "Have you ever interviewed someone before? Do you know what format you're going to do? Who is going to edit it?"

Slightly offended and a little overwhelmed, Owen answered, "Yes, I know what I'm doing. I interviewed a few people in order to get my degree. The rest, I have no clue about, and to any other question you come up with."

"Well, you have my number and I'll help any way that I can," Cameron responded warmly. "Send me your address and I'll send more than enough equipment for you to use."

"That's nice of you." Suspicious, Owen asked, "How do I know you or your aunt won't turn up on our doorstep?"

With a tinge of regret in his voice, Cameron said, "I won't tell Aunt Lexi where he is. He left us for a reason. Us showing up would just make things worse, but maybe you could convince him to call us sometime? We do care about him and we're worried about him."

"Let's hope he doesn't get too upset when I tell him I talked to you." Owen scanned the edge of the woods for any sign of Alex.

Cameron sighed. "He'll get over it."

"I should go before he comes back." Owen stood and stretched. "It was great talking to you. I'll text you my mailing address in a minute."

"Thanks for calling." Cameron chuckled. "Finding out Alex slept with his uncle was the laugh I needed today."

Owen shook his head. "We're never going to live that down, are we?"

"Nope," Cameron said merrily. "Talk to you later. Bye!"

# A WALK IN THE WOODS

**A**LEX STEPPED INTO the familiar woods, a half-acre of trees, underbrush, and various other plants that the small woodland creatures called home. It had been years since he walked these familiar worn paths from town to his Uncle Terry's house and back. Then, after Owen left for school, he wandered these trails for something to do when he was waiting for his Uncle Terry to come back.

Feeling the cool damp air of the forest and the afternoon sunlight filtering down through the leaves, he felt the weight of his decisions weighing down on him. *When Owen left for school, I wrote Uncle Terry off. I ruined my friendships with Dennis, Billy, and so many others.* He stopped at a split in the path. *I ruined my relationships with both Owen and Cameron. Then I had my mother and sister arrested.* His bottom lip trembled. *I fucking use people and throw them away!*

He took the path on the right. It led away from town. *The two people who should have cared the most about me when I got hit by a car couldn't be bothered.* A cool breeze brushed over his skin and danced in his hair. *The two people who should have hated me the most have taken me into their homes.* He continued on the winding dirt path. *Hell, even Carlos looked concerned when he growled at me that he hoped I got better soon.*

He pulled his phone out and sent a quick text to Cameron.

[ALEX: Sorry I've been MIA. I'm okay. Just trying to get my head on straight. I'll call you later. Promise.]

He headed deeper into the woods. Memories of the last time he was in these woods resurfaced. He was trying to lose himself in them back then, too. Owen was gone. He hated his Uncle Terry for taking him away and not coming back for him. His mom and sister told him he had to find his own way after being evicted from yet another home.

He was walking these trails with everything he owned crammed into a backpack. He was trying to build up the courage to go to his Uncle Terry's house. He was so angry that Uncle Terry took Owen away and hadn't come back. He was angry at Owen for leaving and pissed that he let his phone get shut off so he couldn't call Owen.

*Pride.* Alex stopped in a small clearing. *I was too fucking stubborn and proud to ask for help.* He looked around. *I was sleeping on a park bench with everything I owned in a backpack. That's where Emilio found me when he was going for his evening jog.* He let out a humorless

laugh. *He took me in. I found out he liked dick and then I ended up being the biggest dick in the world.*

Alex leaned against a tree. His eyes stung with tears. Alex kicked the ground. *He's how I started doing porn.*

*Showered and dressed, Alex went looking for Emilio. He didn't know much about the man other than he had been the English teacher at his high school until this past year. No one knew much about him. When he moved to take the teaching job, he had a high fence built to keep out prying eyes.*

*The only time he was seen in town was when it was work-related, wearing a pressed white dress shirt that was a size too big and loose midnight-black dress pants and round glasses. The only thing that he changed was his tie, though it was always a solid color.*

*"Feel better after a shower?" Emilio asked from the couch when he saw Alex emerge from the hallway.*

*Alex shifted from foot to foot in the doorway. He tried to reconcile the stoic man he knew as Mr. Ruiz who rarely smiled or showed any personality with the bright and smiling man wearing a tight anime tee that showed off his muscular arms and fashionably distressed jeans sitting there with his shoulder-length black hair pulled up into a topknot.*

*"Yeah, I do. Thanks." Alex stood there, not knowing what to do. "I'll be out of your hair in the morning."*

*Emilio patted the spot next to him. "Stay as long as you need." Alex hesitantly took the seat. "Do you want to tell me why you were sleeping in the park?"*

*"I, uh," Alex looked down at his hands running through each other, "I got evicted again and my mom and sis said I was on my own now that I'm eighteen."*

*Emilio put his hand on Alex's fidgeting hands. "What about your Uncle Terry?"*

*"I can't go to him. It's, um, complicated," Alex squeaked out. "I don't have any place to go yet."*

*Emilio used his other hand to lift Alex's chin. "You can stay here as long as you need to. Under one condition." He smiled. "You have to keep my secret."*

*"Your secret?" Alex questioned. "That you wear normal clothes behind closed doors?"*

*Emilio laughed. "That, I could I give a fuck about." Alex was taken back by his cursing. "Relax, Alex. I'm a normal person despite what those ignorant fucks of this town say." He put his arm around Alex. "I'm not your teacher anymore and I don't work for the school anymore. In fact, I'm moving soon. If you want, you can come with me."*

*"I heard you quit. Rumor was you were being deported." Alex looked at him. "What are you really doing?"*

*Emilio ruffled Alex's hair. "Glad to see you know I'm from this country. My father is Japanese-American and my mother is Mexican-American." He put his arm back around Alex. "I spent the last five years working at that shit school, working my fingers to the bone while getting paid shit."*

*"I think we have different definitions of being paid shit." Alex looked around. "This place is really nice."*

*Emilio gave Alex's shoulder a squeeze. "Luckily, I found a really nice property management company that rented me this place pretty cheap. They even put up that fence for me." Emilio pulled his hand away. "The truth is, I've been supplementing my income for a while now by making fan content." Alex looked at him in confusion. "Sex. People subscribe to see me having sex with other content makers and doing other stuff."*

*"Oh." It took a minute before it hit Alex. "Oh!"*

*"That's why I quit." Emilio laughed. "I make more money doing fan content in a month than I do all year teaching, and I can make even more if I do it full time."*

*Shyly, Alex asked, "Do you think I could make money doing it?"*

*"A young sexy thing like you?" Emilio gave him a once-over. "Yes, if you can put in the work. It's not just filming yourself having sex. There's a lot of work and you have to develop a tough skin." He gave Alex a stern look. "I can teach you, but is this the future that you really want?"*

*Soberly, Alex asked, "What kind of future do I have here?" He shrugged. "You've been doing it without anyone around here finding out."*

*"Okay." Thinking, Emilio bit his lip. "We'll start with the technical stuff first. Editing, filming, and promoting. If you're still up for it after that, then we'll get into the actual sex. Deal?"*

*Alex smiled hopefully. "Deal."*

The sound of a text notification brought Alex out of his thoughts. Pushing off the tree, he headed back to the house. Pulling out his phone, he saw the notification was a text from Cameron. Feeling guilty and fearful of what Cameron messaged back, he tucked his phone back into his pocket.

*I need to fix things between me and him.* Alex stepped out of the woods. *I need to fix things with me and everyone.* Alex crossed the field to the house. *I can start with Owen.* He opened the door to see an angry Owen waiting for him. *Shit. What did I do now?*

# HOW DO YOU WEAR THIS?

**O**WEN STOOD WITH his arms crossed over his chest, glaring at Alex. "Where the hell have you been?"

"I went for a walk in the woods to clear my head," Alex answered, dumbfounded. "Where did you think I went?"

Uncrossing his arms, Owen held up his phone. "I talked to Cameron. He said you left a week ago and you've been avoiding his texts and calls."

Knowing Owen deserved the truth, Alex began, "When I flew here, I needed some time to myself…" Alex paused. He looked curiously at Owen. "Wait. How did you get Cameron's number or he get yours?"

Uncomfortable, Owen admitted, "He kept calling while you were in the shower, so I answered." Owen chewed on the inside of his cheek. "We exchanged numbers, and I talked to him while you were in the woods."

"What the hell?" Alex pulled out his cell and read the text from Cameron aloud, "Thank you for texting. I'm glad you're okay. I talked to your uncle today. I'm going to yell at you with love. Call me later."

The anger in Owen's voice turned sympathetic. "He was worried. I'm worried." He moved to stand in front of Alex. Putting a hand on his shoulder, Owen said, "Don't you see that we care about you?"

"It's hard." Alex tucked his phone away. He saw the concern etched into Owen's face. "I have a lot of baggage to unpack and a lot of people to apologize to." Alex hesitated a moment, then pulled Owen into a hug. "I'm sorry." His voice choked with tears, he said, "I never should have let my mother turn me against you. I never should have hated you and cut you out of my life."

Owen returned the hug. "I'm sorry, too." He squeezed Alex tighter. "We should have told you what was going on. I should have taken you with me."

"I wouldn't have believed you," Alex confessed. "I wish we could start over."

Owen pulled back to look at Alex. "Couldn't we? What's stopping us? Don't we deserve a second chance?"

"I'd like that." Alex's eyes welled with tears. "The truth is, I never stopped loving you." Alex's breath hitched. "Do you know how many times I wished I could pick up the phone and call you?"

Owen cupped his cheek. "Probably as many times as I wanted you to, as many times as I wished I could do the same."

"When I landed, I checked into a hotel instead of coming here," Alex continued his explanation from

earlier. "I was scared you'd turn me away. I drove around for hours before I mustered up the courage to knock on your door."

Owen laughed. "Our door, and you're lucky I didn't shoot you on sight."

"I would have deserved it," Alex laughed along with him. Growing serious, he asked, "What did you and Cameron talk about?"

Owen pulled Alex over to the couch with him. "He told me you were hotel hopping, that you couldn't find work, that you were less than enthusiastic about waking up to see him, his aunt, and his new boyfriend there." He patted Alex's knee. "He thinks the interview is a good idea, and he's sending equipment."

"Why do the people I hurt the most care the most about me?" Alex asked, wiping away a tear.

Owen chewed his lower lip. "Because we know deep down you're a good person." He let out a huff. "Enough emotional baggage. You need to put away your things and get settled in. The entire dresser is yours." He gave Alex's leg a squeeze. "I should figure out what we're going to have for dinner."

"Let's go out to eat," Alex suggested. "They've kept you a prisoner here. I'm setting you free."

"Alex," Owen was about to argue but changed his mind. "Okay. I'll email my attorney instead."

Alex shook his head. "Don't. Let's tell them in person Monday morning." Working his jaw, he explained, "Something doesn't feel right that you've been going through all this and they haven't stopped it."

"They… they said they did everything they could." Owen paused. He cocked his head at Alex. "They did everything they could, right?"

Standing up, Alex shrugged. "I don't know, but it seems strange that this has lasted this long." He pulled Owen up. "Come, keep me company while I put away my things and tell me I'm doing it wrong."

"You still don't fold things?" Owen grinned. "Come on. I'll make sure you fold your underwear correctly."

Alex snorted. "Like I wear underwear." Back in the bedroom, Alex opened his bag and dumped the clothes on the bed. "You fold, I put away."

"Do you even try to fold your clothes?" Owen pulled a shirt from the pile, looked at it, and raised an eyebrow as he read it, "Your dad is my cardio?"

Alex snatched the shirt. "I think I should wear that to dinner."

"No." Owen snatched the shirt back. "We're going to get enough stares and whispers." Brushing out the wrinkles, Owen joked, "Too bad there's not one that says my uncle is my cardio."

Laughing, Alex carefully took the folded shirt. "I'll have one made." He put the shirt away. "How do you know that cop? That Flynn dude?"

"Xavier?" Owen folded another shirt. "We use to fuck." He held out the shirt to Alex, who stood there. "I'm kidding. He's straight. I know him from college." Alex took the shirt. "He and a few others at the station have been trying to get those good ole boys out."

Curiously, Alex asked, "Have you, you know, dated anyone?"

"Lately? No." Owen held up a black G-string. "How do I fold this?"

Alex snatched it from him. "You don't." He threw it back at Owen. "You wear it tonight."

"Not happening. I want more than a string between my cheeks." Owen tossed the underwear aside and picked up a pair of shorts. "I thought you said you didn't wear underwear."

Alex took the folded shorts. "I was joking. Of course, I wear underwear. For protection."

"Protection?" Owen handed Alex another folded shirt.

Putting the shirt away, Alex explained. "Yeah, from zippers. Once zipped twice shy."

"Ouch." Owen held up a red garment with multiple straps and a pouch. "Do I need to ask?"

Alex took it and put it aside. "That gets hung up in the closet."

"How do you even put that on?" Owen handed him more clothes.

"Carefully." Alex laughed. Putting the clothes away, he nervously asked, "So you haven't dated anyone?"

Smiling to himself, Owen said, "I didn't say that." He handed Alex a stack of shirts. "I was no angel, and neither were you. Let's leave it at that."

"Okay." Alex put away the shirts. "But if you had to say, like, a number?" Owen threw a jock strap into his face. "Fine. I get it." He folded the jock, then put it in the drawer.

Owen playfully punched him. "You jerk! You do know how to fold your clothes!"

"Of course I do." Alex snatched a pair of jeans from the pile and brushed out the wrinkles. "I just don't like to." Owen punched him slightly harder in the arm. "Ouch! What was that for?"

Owen handed him the last of the folded clothes. "Because for years I had to fold your clothes and put them away for you before…"

"I liked that you took care of me." Alex put the clothes away. He looked guiltily at Owen. "Is this a bad time to tell you I knew how to cook all this time?"

Owen grabbed Alex and threw him onto the bed. "Asshole!"

"I'm sorry!" Alex laughed, rolling around the bed with Owen. "I'll do the laundry from now on!"

Straddling Alex, Owen rose up and glared down. "You know how to do laundry? You jerk!" He grabbed a pillow and hit Alex with it. "How many of my clothes did you ruin before I just did it myself?!" He hit Alex with the pillow. "You ruined my favorite jeans!"

"I'm sorry!" Alex laughed, snatching the pillow away. Growing serious, he said, "I meant it. I liked that you cared enough to do those things for me."

Owen brushed Alex's hair from his face. "Of course, I cared about you. I still do." He playfully flicked Alex on the forehead. "But I didn't like doing all the cooking and cleaning!"

"Okay! Okay! I said I was sorry!" Alex took hold of Owen by the hips and rolled them, so he was on top. "How about instead of hitting me, you spank me instead?"

Owen pretended to struggle. "You'd like that too much."

"And you wouldn't?" Alex asked seductively.

Stopping his struggling, Owen asked, "What are we doing?" Alex pulled back with concern. "Sucker!" Owen flipped them so he was on top and pinned Alex's hands by his head. "Okay, seriously. What are we doing? Are we flirting? Are we fighting?"

"Both?" Alex wiggled his hips. "You do have my rooster crowing."

Owen rolled off Alex with a groan. "As much as I would like to, um, choke your chicken, I think we should take it slow. We both have a lot of baggage."

"I'll wear the red strappy thing that goes in the closet." Alex cringed at Owen's disapproving look. "Okay, fine." He shot up his arm with his index finger extended. "I reserve the right to flirt, be protective, and touch you inappropriately whenever I want."

Shaking his head, Owen smiled. "Fine. Why don't you go call Cameron? I'll shower and get ready. Then we can go to town and walk around and make people uncomfortable before we grab something to eat?"

"Fine," Alex grumbled, sitting up. "I didn't bring any lube, anyways."

Getting up off the bed, Owen teased, "Nightstand." He turned to see Alex moving toward the nightstand. He jumped on top of Alex, screaming, "No!"

"Too late!" Alex shouted triumphantly. "What's this?" he asked, pulling out a silicone latex cock and balls. "And this?" He pulled out a masturbation sleeve. "Look! I found the lube!" He held up the bottle. "Almost empty. Put lube on the grocery list."

Owen smacked the lube out of Alex's hand. "That does not go on the grocery list. I buy that when I go to the adult store in the city."

"What do you do with the dildo?" Alex teased, waving it around.

Owen rolled off Alex, snatched it, and dropped it back in the drawer before closing it. "You're the adult film star. You tell me."

"I could show you," Alex said with a wink.

Owen pointed to the door. "Out! Call Cameron!"

"Fine." Alex rolled off the bed. On his way out of the room, he mumbled under his breath, "We're getting so much lube."

Shaking his head in amusement, Owen thought to himself, *That's the Alex I remember. The fun, silly guy that made me laugh.* He picked up the black G-string from the bed. *How do people wear these? It looks like an eye patch.*

# 13

# YELLING WITH LOVE

**A**LEX PACED THE living room, looking at Cameron's contact information on his screen. He chewed on his cheek and lip dreading what Cameron was going to say to him. *He's going to chew my ass out, then hand it to me.* He sat down on the sofa. He looked up at the picture of his Uncle Terry. *Asshole. You should have told me.*

With a deep breath, he gathered his courage. He hit the call button.

"It's about damn time!" Cameron answered. "Hold on, let me take this into the other room." He heard Cameron say to someone, "It's Alex. He finally called. Don't give me that look." He heard Cameron stomping away in a huff. "Okay, I can yell at you in peace now."

Alex winced. "If this is a bad time, I can call back."

"Don't you dare hang up this phone," Cameron scolded. "What were you thinking, leaving in the middle of the night and not telling anyone?! And how dare you not answer my calls and texts?! Where the fuck were you for the past week?! I talked to Owen, and that's a whole nother discussion we're going to have!"

Alex waited a second before asking, "Are you done? Or do you need to yell some more questions at me?"

"Smart ass," Cameron snapped. "Do you want me to get Aunt Lexi on three-way? I'm sure she has more."

Alex shrank into the sofa. "Please don't." Alex pulled his knees up to his chest. "Okay, let's go in order. As for what I was thinking about leaving, I knew if I didn't leave while everyone was gone, you guys wouldn't have let me." He sighed. "I had to leave, Cameron. Hiding at Lexi's place was a painful reminder of how bad I fucked up my life and hurt you. I had to leave."

"I'll accept that," Cameron said coldly. "Go on, and it better be good."

Alex smiled. He knew the only reason Cameron was upset was because he cared. "I needed to step away from everything. I was planning on coming straight here, but when I landed, I, I don't know, it hit me where I was going and I got scared. I checked into a hotel and tried to get my head on right. If I talked to you then, I don't know. I needed to be by myself, with my own thoughts."

"I don't like it, but I get it," Cameron conceded.

Alex looked back toward the bedroom. "I don't know why I came here. It felt like the only place I could go, the place that I needed to go, because Owen and I have unfinished business."

"Owen, your first kiss," Cameron clarified.

"Yes." Alex smiled at the memory.

Cameron continued, "Owen, your first boyfriend."

"Yeah." Alex hugged his knees tighter to his chest.

Cameron added, "Owen, your first time."

"Oh, yeah." Alex grinned.

With humor in his voice, Cameron said, "Owen, your uncle."

"Yeah," Alex said dreamily, before snapping, "Hey! He's only my uncle by marriage!"

Laughing, Cameron said, "I know. He told me." Regaining his composure, he said, "He seems to really care for you." Cameron paused. "Are you okay, Alex? He told me about your mother and sister."

"Cameron," Alex tried to gather his thoughts, "sometimes the truth hurts. Coming back here, my eyes were opened to a lot of truths." He felt a pain in his heart. "My mom and sister are not good people. They have been putting Owen through hell. I can't believe that they might have…"

Cameron quietly said, "I know."

"They have been putting Owen through hell for no other reason than that they want to, and it helps them raise money in some stupid crowdfunding scheme." Alex shook his head. "I don't understand how his attorney hasn't stopped it."

Cameron offered, "I can have Aunt Lexi's people look into it."

"Could you? That would be great." Alex felt an unbearable weight pressing down on him. "Cameron, I'm sorry."

Confused, Cameron asked, "For? This is you, after all. I need you to be a little more specific."

"For everything." A tear ran down his cheek. "For treating you like an accessory. For cheating on you.

For all the lies. For not loving you like I should and basically being a horrible boyfriend to you."

There was a brief silence before Cameron said, "I forgive you."

"What can I do to make things right?" Alex asked, tears running down his face.

Cameron's answer was heartfelt. "Be a better person going forward."

"Do you think Dennis, Billy, and everyone else I hurt will listen to my apologies?" Alex wiped at the tears. "They don't have to forgive me. I just want them to know I'm sorry."

"I think they will," Cameron answered. "Especially after they see your tell-all interview on Lexi's new network."

"Do you think you and Lexi can help him?" Alex glanced back again toward the bedroom. "I was going to ask, when we had it all done and had something to show her." He looked at his Uncle Terry's picture. "Owen put his dreams on hold because of my family."

"Me, Aunt Lexi, and Billy's boyfriend, Jordan will help him," Cameron answered.

Alex hugged his legs tighter. "Jordan is someone else I need to apologize to."

"Hey," Cameron said, snapping Alex out of his melancholy. "You apologized to me, and I accepted it. Take that win. I'll talk to everyone else. By the time you show up at Hunter's and Mark's wedding, everyone will be ready to forgive you."

A knot twisted in Alex's gut. "I don't think it would be appropriate for me to go to their wedding.

Besides, I don't think Hunter really wants me there, and I know everyone else doesn't."

"I know for a fact that Hunter wants you there," Cameron argued. "As for anyone else, fuck them. It's his and Mark's wedding. Not theirs."

Alex smiled. "I'll think about it." He sighed. "Cameron, how come you're doing all this for me? How can you forgive me so easily?"

"It wasn't that easy," Cameron laughed. "I was angry at you for a very long time. Aunt Lexi helped me see that had you not done what you did, I wouldn't have ended up with Carlos."

Alex groaned, "He hates me with a passion."

"No, I think he wants to. I think he's jealous, and that's on him, and on me. Not you. I think he really wants to like you." Cameron sighed. "Anyways, when I got that call from the hospital and found out about the hotel hopping, seeing you trying to contact your mom, and the look on your face, I saw you were hurting. Not physically because you were on some good medication, but you were hurting so bad emotionally."

Cameron took in a deep breath and exhaled. "Alex, that's when I realized I still loved you, even if I wasn't in love with you. I still cared what happened to you. I still do. When you were lying in that hospital bed, I got a glimpse of the guy you were when we first started dating. You just needed a second chance."

"Cameron, I have to confess something." Alex closed his eyes and prepared for the repercussions of what he was about to say. "I don't think I was ever really in love with you, but I did grow to love you."

"Because you're in love with your uncle?" Cameron teased.

Alex groaned. "Can we get over that already?" He double-checked to make sure Owen wasn't around. "But yes, it was because I was in love with Owen. I think I still am."

"Think or know?" Cameron prodded.

Alex thought for a moment. "Think. I'll know once we get all these old feelings worked out."

"Well, figure it out." Cameron paused. "Hold on." Away from the phone, he yelled, "I will be as long as I want to!" Back to Alex, he said, "I need to get going, but we're gathering the equipment Owen will need. Do you think you can handle the lighting and editing?"

Alex put his feet down on the floor. "Yeah. Thank you. You should go. I don't want to be the reason you and Carlos fight."

"Are you kidding? We have our best sex after we fight. It's like foreplay," Cameron said devilishly. Growing serious, Cameron said, "I expect you to call me at least once a week and anytime you need to. Day or night. Same goes for Owen. Understood?"

Alex stood up. He turned around to see Owen standing in the hallway wearing one of his shirts, a black retro-style tee that had a unicorn on it, prancing with a rainbow arching between two clouds that read, "Masc for Masc." "I'll let him know. Talk to you later. Bye." Alex set the phone down. "Hey."

"I didn't mean to interrupt." Owen rubbed his arms uncomfortably. "I hope you don't mind. The shirt, that is. I saw it when we were folding your clothes and I liked it."

Alex crossed the room to Owen. "Not one bit." Alex chuckled. "That's actually not my shirt, it's Cameron's. I must have packed it by accident." Smiling, Alex said, "I don't think he'd mind. It looks good on you."

"I, uh, guess we should get going," Owen said nervously.

Alex took Owen's hand. "Remember, we need to pick up lube." He winked at Owen. "Lots and lots of lube."

# 14

# GIVING THEM SOMETHING TO TALK ABOUT

**O**WEN FELT EVERYONE'S judging eyes on them as they walked the streets of town. He saw them murmuring and whispering. Some were even bold enough to point. While it made him uncomfortable, it didn't seem to bother Alex one bit. He strode confidently in a black crop top and jeans so tight Owen had to carry his cell and wallet.

"You had to dress so…" Owen struggled to find the right word.

Alex looked at him with a grin. "Sexy?"

"Obvious," Owen corrected.

Alex put his arm around Owen's shoulders. "You're one to speak wearing a shirt with a picture of a unicorn and rainbow with 'Masc for Masc' on it."

Owen stopped. "You said it looked cute on me."

Alex tugged him along. "It does. That's why Cameron isn't getting it back."

"I can't believe I let you out of the house wearing that," Owen said in disbelief before erupting in laughter. "I guess we're giving them something to talk about, huh?"

Alex led them into one of the local taverns. "Exactly." He smiled at the scandalized teenage hostess. "Two for dinner."

"Um," she hesitantly grabbed two menus, looked at the map on her podium, then said, "Follow me." Owen tried to ignore the eyes of the other guests watching them cross the dining room to their booth. She sat the menus down, nervously said, "Your server will be with you in a moment," then rushed off.

Owen slipped in on one side. "That was odd."

"Was it?" Alex slipped in on the other side and picked up the menu. "What's good here?"

Owen glanced down at the menu. "I have no idea. I haven't eaten in this town for obvious reasons."

"What I don't get is why my mom and sister are harassing you so badly," Alex commented while looking over the menu. "What made them turn you into public enemy number one?"

Owen looked up from the menu. "I was an easy villain for them to raise money to defeat." He let Alex take that in before adding, "They know about the company. They tried to force their way in there, but there's a clause in the ownership that gives the employees first right to buy." Owen looked back down at his menu. "They don't have the power in Vista that they have in Springfield."

"How much property do we actually own?" Alex looked around for their server. He watched a new table be sat, and a server immediately greet them.

Owen looked back up at Alex. "A lot. We own all the rental properties in this town. Houses, shops, and restaurants. When everyone was about to lose their homes and businesses, Terry bought them up and rented them back to everyone. He saved this town from becoming a ghost town."

"Like this place?" Alex asked, watching another table that was sat after them being served drinks.

"Yes." Owen looked around. He shook his head, defeated. "I told you, getting something to eat in town was a bad idea."

Alex stood. "Stay here." He strolled over to the hostess stand. The young lady looked at him nervously. "Have the manager come to our table, and when you tell him who is asking for him, tell him it's his landlords, and we're debating on whether to renew this place's lease."

"Um, okay." The young lady rushed off.

When Alex returned to his seat, Owen asked, "What did you do?"

"I made it known that it might not be a good idea to give your landlords bad service." Alex smiled.

A portly man with a neatly trimmed back beard came to the table. "I'm the manager on duty. I understand you two wished to speak to me."

"Yes." Alex pointed at another table that was just seated, being greeted by their server. "We've been here for about ten minutes and haven't had anyone

greet us, or even acknowledge our existence while tables around us are being greeted within seconds."

The man gave his best fake sympathetic smile. "We reserve the right to refuse service to someone who has their mother arrested and someone who stole her inheritance." He motioned to the door. "If you'll, please, leave before I call the authorities and have you arrested for loitering."

"We'll leave." Alex stood up. "We'll be back, though. When it's time to inspect our property. When it's time to renew your lease. Of course, I don't see that happening."

Owen stood and put a hand on Alex's arm. "Alex, don't cause a scene."

"Get the fuck out," the manager snarled.

Alex pursed his lips and bobbed his head back and forth. "I had my mother and sister arrested. You think I wouldn't be a landlord from hell to you?" Alex raised his voice. "That goes for all of you!" The restaurant went silent.

"If you're renting in this town, you're probably renting from Owen and me! We don't have to renew your leases! If you want to believe the lies my mother and sister have been spreading, that's on you! Know this: We will not rent to people who treat us like shit!" Alex scanned the restaurant. "My Uncle Terry was the hero who saved this town. I'm the villain who will watch it burn to prove a point."

"Boy, you need to go." The manager reached out to take Alex by the arm, but Owen blocked him by stepping in front. "And take your fucking slut with you. Fucking freaks."

Owen clenched his fist in anger. Instead of striking anyone, he pulled out his cell and put it to his ear after dialing a number. When the call connected, he spoke loud enough for everyone to hear. "James, I'm sorry to bother you at home, but I wanted to let you know as soon as possible that we will not be auto-renewing the leases in Springfield. Yes, we can start entertaining those commercial offers. We'll go over the full details Monday. Have a good night." Owen tucked away his cell. "Spread that like you guys spread the lies about me." He took Alex by the hand. "Come on. Let's get food from a place that doesn't have a C rating from the health inspector."

"That was a nice bluff," Alex commented once they were outside.

Owen tightened his grip on Alex's hand. "It wasn't a bluff." He led them back to Alex's car. "Vista is twenty minutes away. We've had a ton of inquiries for rentals. Not everyone who works in the city wants to live there." They stopped at Alex's rental. "Most of our current renters are three or more months behind because they pay when they want."

"That ends now." Alex held out his hand. "Keys?"

Owen hipped-bumped Alex away. "I'm driving. There's a place in Vista I want to try out."

"Vista?" Alex questioned, getting in the passenger side. "Why are we driving all the way out there?"

"After word gets out about our little scene," Owen slipped in behind the wheel, "I'm pretty sure we need to go to Vista to get food that won't be poisoned." He shifted uncomfortably in the seat. "How do you wear these?"

Alex gave Owen a curious look. "Wear what?"

"G-stings." Owen fastened his seat belt. "I can't imagine thongs would be any more comfortable."

Alex grinned. "You're wearing one of my G-strings?"

Owen started the car and pulled out of the parking spot. "Yeah, that black eye patch-looking thing. I either have it on wrong or it's too small for me."

"Owen, remember how we agreed to take it slow?" Alex looked at Owen with lust.

Suspiciously, Owen said, "Yeah."

"When we get home," Alex growled, "I'm pulling that G-string off with my teeth."

# 15

# DO BULLS MOO?

"**H**URRY UP! HURRY up!" Alex bounced from foot to foot on the front porch. "If you don't hurry, I'm going to pee in the yard!"

Unlocking the door, Owen pushed open the door. "Here." He laughed as Alex rushed by him. "You shouldn't have drank so much soda!" he called after him.

"Fuck these tight pants!" Alex shouted from the bathroom

Owen locked the door, then reset the alarms. "Oh, you're pretty fuckable in those tight pants."

"Oh, God! That feels good!" Alex proclaimed from the bathroom.

Owen shook his head. "If you piss on the floor, you're cleaning it up!" He headed down the hall. "You better have lifted the seat too!"

"I'll wipe it!" Alex shouted back.

Leaning against the door frame to the bathroom, Owen casually asked, "How are you still peeing?"

"I had four sodas," Alex sighed in relief as the last drips hit the water. "How are your eyes not floating?"

Owen went to the sink. "I peed at the restaurant. Now wipe the seat and brush your teeth. It's time for bed."

"It's like nine." Alex tucked his dick back in his pants. "I don't want to go to bed this early." He wiped the seat with toilet paper, then flushed everything down. "Let's watch a movie or something."

Owen handed Alex his toothbrush. "Brush your teeth. You had garlic." He began brushing his teeth. He leaned on the sink, causing his shirt to rise up and his jeans to slide down his hips. He spit. "I said go to bed, not sleep."

"Oh!" Alex exclaimed, seeing the thin black waistband exposed. He furiously started scrubbing his teeth. "Do you know how long it's been?" he said around his toothbrush. "Months."

Owen rinsed his mouth, then spit. "Try years." He wiped his mouth with a hand towel. "I know we agreed to go slow, and you were joking about pulling these off me with your teeth—"

"I wasn't joking." Alex quickly rinsed and spit. "My rooster is crowing for you." He moved behind Owen and took him in his arms. "I know we have a lot of baggage to unpack, but I can't go another day without the taste of you on my lips."

Owen reached back and ran his fingers through Alex's hair. "Tonight showed me I'm stronger with you. I wouldn't have had the courage to do what I did if you weren't by my side." He put his hands on top of Alex's. "We've lost so much time to other people's bullshit. Let's not lose anymore because of our own." He turned in Alex's arms to face him. "We're better together, and despite our baggage, we both know we're going to end up together. Your rooster crows for me like my bull moos for you."

"Do bulls moo?" Alex questioned. "Actually, what sound do bulls make?"

Owen rubbed his groin against Alex. "Why don't you get me naked and find out?"

"I think you should work for it." Alex gave him a light kiss. "Actually, you have to. I need help getting out of these pants. They are really tight."

Owen slipped out of Alex's arms. "Oh, I'll get you out of those jeans, alright." Laughing, he pulled Alex to the bedroom. First, he pulled Alex's shirt off, then pushed him onto the bed. "Unbutton your jeans." Owen pulled off Alex's shoes and socks then kicked off his own shoes.

"I think you might be horny." Alex unbuttoned his pants and lowered his zipper. He pushed his pants down while Owen tugged at his pants legs. "I bet you never thought it would ever be this hard to get me out of my pants."

Owen fell back on his ass when he finally pulled Alex's pants free. He looked up to see a naked Alex standing over him. "No underwear?"

"Do you think I could wear underwear in those pants?" Alex pulled Owen to his feet and pulled his shirt off in one swift motion. He ran his hands over Owen's chest, through the small patch of chest hair between his pecs, then down his soft belly to the top

of his pants. He popped open the top button. He looked Owen in the eyes. Softly he said, "Oh, Owen."

Their mouths crashed together. Hungry and savage, they ravaged each other's mouths. Owen's hands freely roamed over Alex, rediscovering his body. Owen moaned, "You're far from that skinny guy I left behind." He started kissing along Alex's neck.

"I love how your body feels pressed next to mine." Alex shoved Owen's pants down his hips. "Fuck, you're beautiful." Alex began kissing his way down Owen's chest as he dropped to his knees. Helping Owen out of his jeans, he smiled up at Owen. "I can't believe how sexy you look in my G-string."

Owen blushed. "I do not. I don't have the body for it."

"Yes, you do." Alex took hold of the waistband and began tugging it down, lifting the pouch over Owen's hard-on. He spun Owen around, took hold of the top of the G-string, then began tugging it down until it fell down his legs. He whistled. "Your ass sure did plump up."

Owen jumped and yelped when Alex nibbled on his ass cheek. "You bit me!"

"I'm going to do more than bite you." Alex kissed the spot he nipped. "I've learned a lot more since the last time we did this."

Owen leaned over the bed and spread his legs when he felt Alex's hands pull his cheeks apart. "Show me, don't tell me."

Owen gasped at the swipe of Alex's tongue along his crevice. He let out low moans and groans from Alex's tongue flicking and running random patterns

over his delicate skin. Alex pulled at Owen's cheeks, trying to delve deeper into him. Owen pushed back, needing him to do so.

Alex pushed a finger into Owen. "Damn, you're tight."

"Then loosen me up," Owen snapped. "Better yet," Owen turned around and pulled Alex to his feet, "let me show you what I learned."

Owen dropped to his knees. With one hand holding Alex's cock up and the other on Alex's muscular thigh to steady him, Owen took one of Alex's balls in his mouth. Alex's hands dug into his shoulders to try to steady himself. Owen moved from one smooth orb to the other, while his hand moved across Alex's dick.

"Fuck, yeah, Owen." Alex tossed his head back. He fisted Owen's hair. "I'm going to pound your tight ass into the mattress."

Owen licked up the familiar trek of Alex's shaft. He looked up into Alex's eyes as he took the head of Alex's cock in his mouth. He watched pleasure spread across Alex's face as he slowly took most of Alex's length into his mouth.

"You learned a few new things, too," Alex moaned, running his hand through Owen's hair.

Owen closed his eyes and began moving his head back and forth, enjoying the feel of Alex's cock in his mouth. The hard flesh glided along his lips. He gently fondled Alex's balls with his free hand. He pressed his tongue along the underside of Alex's shaft and danced it over his crown.

"I forgot how good your mouth feels." Alex urged Owen farther onto his cock. "I forgot how good you feel." He began pumping his hips in time with Owen's bobs.

Alex's words urged Owen on. He pushed Alex farther into his mouth until he gagged. Owen bobbed and twisted his head. Lust-filled hunger surged through him. His hand moved from Alex's balls to grab Alex's ass. He pulled Alex hard into his mouth, guiding Alex to face fuck him.

With his growing desire, Alex pulled his cock from Owen's mouth. He leaned down and crushed his mouth against Owen's, invading Owen's mouth with his tongue. He pulled Owen up to sit on the bed. He moved his hands down to spread Owen's legs.

"My turn," Alex growled into the kiss, taking Owen's cock in his hand.

Stroking Owen's dick as he dropped to his knees, Alex lowered his head down into Owen's lap. He kissed the tip of Owen's cock. "I missed you, old friend." He then swallowed Owen down to the base. He let out a groan of satisfaction at the feel of Owen's cock in his throat. His hands moved up and over Owen's body,

Alex took his time sucking Owen, enjoying the taste and feel of Owen's hardness in his mouth. Owen was a leaker the last time they played. To Alex's delight, he still was, and was leaving his sweet sticky trail over Alex's tongue.

Alex used his exploring hand over Owen's chest to gauge his pace. When Owen's breathing quickened and grew erratic, he slowed down until Owen's

breaths steadied. Then he would bring Owen back ever so close to the edge before pulling him back.

"Either let me cum or get your dick in me," Owen snarled, voice deep and raspy.

Alex let Owen's cock slip from his mouth with a wet pop. "Oh, you're not ready for my dick yet." Alex opened the nightstand and reached in. "And I'm not done making you moan." He pulled out the lube, followed by Owen's dildo. He smiled with wicked satisfaction at Owen's look of curiosity and desire. He hefted Owen's legs up, exposing his hole.

"Tell me if it gets to be too much." Alex kissed Owen's inner thigh. "I never want to hurt you again." He rubbed a lubed finger over Owen's hole. He lightly kissed Owen's ball. "Tell me when you're ready."

Owen leaned back. For a moment, he was tempted to take matters into his own hands, but instead hooked his arms around his legs and pulled them back for Alex. He took a centering breath and let it out. "I'm ready, baby."

Alex rubbed his finger in circles around Owen's hole while planting soft kisses on his cock and balls. He pressed the finger into Owen's tight confines, then pulled it out again. He rubbed his finger over the hole, then pushed it in again with less resistance.

"That's it." Alex pulled his finger out and added a second to rub over Owen's hole. He pushed the two fingers into his hole. "Open up for me." He pulled the two fingers out, rubbed his fingers over the hole, then pushed them in again. "I'm going to make you feel so good," Alex said, with a kiss on Owen's balls.

He repeated the routine until two fingers moved in easily and then repeated the process with a third finger added. He casually drizzled more lube on his fingers while he pushed them in and out of Owen. He felt Owen relaxing and welcoming him in.

He pulled his fingers out when he felt Owen relax enough and picked up the dildo. He slicked up the phallic replica, then placed the latex tip to Owen's entrance. He watched Owen's face as he pushed it into him. He watched the latex cock slip easily into Owen with lustful delight. He was impressed as much as he was aroused.

"Not bad for someone out of practice." Alex kissed along Owen's thighs and balls. He pumped the cock replica in and out of Owen.

Owen moaned, "I need the real thing."

"You'll get it." Alex licked up along Owen's shaft. "You must really want my dick the way you're leaking." He pumped the dildo in and out of Owen. "Do you want my dick, baby?"

Owen's voice was filled with dripping need. "Alex, I need you in me already."

"Okay, baby." Alex slowly pulled the replica from Owen and set it aside. Standing up, he slicked his dick up while Owen moved up on the bed. "This doesn't get you out of giving me a show with that thing sometime." He climbed up on the bed, lifted Owen's legs up, and rested them on his shoulders. "Are you ready?"

Owen put his arms around Alex. "Would you quit treating me like a delicate flower and—" Owen moaned at Alex slipping into him.

"Oh, fuck, you feel good in me." Owen begged, "Fuck me, Alex. Fuck me, please."

"No, baby." Alex pressed his hips flush against Owen. Looking down at him, Alex said, "I'm going to love you."

He covered Owen's mouth with his and began rhythmically thrusting his hips. Owen's legs slipped to wrap around Alex's waist, and his hands came around to pull Alex closer. Alex pumped harder and faster into Owen.

Bodies pressed closed, mouths hungry for one another and Owen's strong arms and legs holding onto him tight, Alex pushed himself relentlessly into Owen. With the carnal act turned passionate, Alex felt it. The need for Owen. To claim him, and, in turn, be claimed by Owen.

Alex's body began to tremble. He kissed Owen harder. Owen clung to him tighter, digging his fingers into Alex's corded back. Alex's release surged forth. He cried out into the kiss, refusing to break his connection with Owen. His body shook with the intensity of a hundred earthquakes. He pushed hard into Owen, grew rigid, then finally collapsed on top of him.

Their kiss turned leisurely and Owen eased his grip on Alex to stroke his broad back. Alex played in Owen's hair. He wiggled his hips, reminding Owen how hard he still was in him. Owen raked his nails up Alex's back, causing him to break the kiss with a gasp.

Alex nuzzled Owen's cheek and growled in his ear, "That was amazing."

"We're not done yet," Owen whispered in his ear. He brought up a hand to the top of Alex's head. "Don't

be a selfish top." He pushed Alex's head down. "You've got more work to do. Don't worry, it won't take long."

Kissing his way down Owen's body, Alex seductively whispered, "We'll see about that." Owen pulled him away by his hair. "Ouch! That hurts!"

"It will not take that long," Owen said sharply. "Understood." He let go of Alex's hair.

Alex winked. "Fine, next time."

Alex smiled at the whimper Owen let out when his cock slipped out. He took Owen's cock between his lips and sucked him down. Slipping a hand under Owen, Alex pressed two fingers into Owen's well-used hole. He moved in time, slipping his fingers in while pulling off Owen's cock, then pulling his fingers out while sucking him back down.

"Oh, Alex." Owen fisted Alex's hair while thrusting his hips up and down. "I told you I wasn't going to last long!" He pulled Alex's head down hard into his crotch while thrusting his hips up. "Alex!"

Owen's cock exploded in Alex's mouth with convulsing jolts. He held Alex's head tight against his groin as what felt like an ocean of his pent-up desire was unleashed. He pumped his cock into Alex's hungry mouth, letting loose a torrent of grunts and groans before letting go and going limp on the bed.

"That was great," Owen sighed. He looked down at Alex grinning at him with his cock in his mouth. "You can pull your fingers out and take my dick out of your mouth now." Alex pulled the fingers from Owen, but left Owen's cock in his mouth. "Don't you—" Before he could finish the threat, Alex moved his mouth along

Owen's cock, causing him to jolt from the sensitivity. He grabbed Alex by the hair. "Not funny! Sensitive!"

Alex let Owen slip from his mouth. "Good to see some things never change." He moved to lay beside Owen. "You taste a little more bitter than I remember."

"Jerk." Owen playfully smacked his chest, then curled up next to him. "I needed that, though."

Alex put his arm around Owen. "I needed you." He kissed the top of Owen's head. "Let me get you a washcloth."

"Not yet." Owen kept him from getting up. "I want to hold you a bit longer in case this is just a dream."

Alex groaned at the sound of pounding on the door. "Who could that be?"

"Let me check." Owen kissed Alex on the cheek. He pulled himself away to grab his phone from his pants. He opened up the security app on his phone and pulled up the cameras. "Why is Xavier here?"

Sitting up in the bed, Alex looked over his shoulder. "Guess we better put pants on and find out."

# 16

## MORNING COFFEE

**A**LEX STOOD AT the counter, making a cup of coffee, when he felt Owen's hands encircle his bare waist. Owen kissed the top of his left shoulder. Resting his head there, he pulled Alex close like a security blanket. Alex put his hand on top of Owen's and closed his eyes, trying to commit everything about the moment to memory.

"Good morning," Owen said softly, breaking the silence.

Alex opened his eyes. "Good morning. I made you coffee."

"Thank you." Owen slowly pulled his hands away, letting his fingers slide over Alex's trim waist. "I remember there being a lot less of you."

Alex laughed. He took the coffee he was making and turned to hand it to Owen. "See what happens when you eat your vegetables?" Taking the coffee, Owen gave him a scathing look. "I started working out, hitting the gym." He curled his left arm up to make his bicep bulge. "Do you like?"

"No," Owen said with a sip of his coffee to hide his smile. "I love it, and I don't believe you're eating your vegetables."

Alex pulled Owen by the hips to him. "Believe it. I even eat kale now."

"Look at you being a grownup," Owen teased, kissing Alex. "Thanks for letting me sleep in. I think that's the first good night's sleep I've had in years."

Alex brushed Owen's hair with his fingers. "I figured you needed it, and before you ask, I already checked on Xavier and Benjamin when he took over for him." Grinning, he asked, "How does it feel to be one-half of the most hated couple in town?"

"Don't remind me." Owen pulled away. "It's not like I wasn't before. Now I just have company." He sat down on the couch. "How long do you think we need off-duty cops parked out front to protect us from the idiots in town?"

Hearing the resignation and fear in Owen's voice, Alex went to him and took him in his arms. "It's going to be okay. If we need to, we can move." He pulled Owen into his arms. "We'll do whatever it takes to keep you safe."

"I am safe as long as I'm with you." Owen sipped his coffee. "What do you want to do today?"

Alex slipped a hand under Owen's shirt. "We can try and get you pregnant." He rubbed Owen's soft belly.

"You know men can't get pregnant." Owen laughed. He put a hand where Alex's hand was under his shirt.

"I guess I'm not the body type you're used to having in your bed."

Alex felt guilt and shame remembering his fight with Billy. "I was such an asshole about things like that." He kissed the top of Owen's head. "I want to bring that up in the interview." He patted Owen's belly. "How about we go over what we want to talk about in the interview?"

"After you get me another cup of coffee." Owen held up his empty cup. "I'm possibly with child after the two rounds last night."

Alex took the cup and gingerly slipped from under Owen. "Do you want kids? Not mine splattering all over you, but I mean, children."

"I never thought about it." Owen shifted to watch Alex in the kitchen. "Do you?"

Fixing Owen's coffee, Alex thought for a moment. "I didn't think it was something I could have, but now," he brought Owen his coffee, "I don't know. I think I do."

"Well," Owen shifted to let Alex return to his spot under him, "we can talk about it. I like the idea of giving some kid a happy home like Terry did for us."

Alex slipped his hand back under Owen's shirt. "I like that idea, too." A notification sounded on Alex's phone. Grabbing it, he read it out loud. "Cameron wants to know if we're free to talk later."

"Yeah." Owen settled back against Alex. "He seems like a nice guy. He seems to really care about you."

Alex sent back a reply of, [Yes, in an hour or so,] then set the phone down. "He is, and I really did him wrong. I hurt a lot of people being the person I was."

"That's who you were, not who you are." Owen set his coffee down. Sitting up, he turned and pulled Alex to rest against his chest. "You can show them that you changed. That's all you can do. You may not be forgiven, but you can at least let people know you are sorry for what you did."

Alex looked at the picture of his Uncle Terry. "Not everyone will know."

"Him?" Owen followed Alex's eyes to the picture. "He knows." Owen patted Alex's hard stomach. "Trust me, he knows."

# OWEN AND CAMERON

OWEN USED THE excuse of being on camera to sit close to Alex when, in reality, he needed to draw comfort from Alex as they waited for the video call to connect. He hadn't expected their conversation with Cameron to be on camera. Had he known, he would have dressed better, maybe run a brush through his hair.

"Stop worrying," Alex whispered, shoulder-bumping Owen. "It's just Cameron."

Owen bit his tongue. *Just Cameron, your ex-fiancé, and the guy helping us do this stupid interview that no one will ever see.* Owen sighed. "I would have tried to look presentable if I knew it was a video call."

"You look fine." They both jumped at Cameron's voice coming from Alex's phone. He smiled at them, wearing an oversized tee and a backward-turned ball cap. "This is really an informal meeting so we can discuss the interview and for me to get to know you."

Alex put an arm around Owen. "Cameron, meet Owen. Owen, meet Cameron."

"Nice to put a face with the voice and stories." Owen smiled nervously.

Cameron said sweetly, "Same." He brought his face closer to the screen. "You two fucked, didn't you?"

"We… How… No… Oh, my god," Owen stammered out before putting his face in his hands, embarrassed.

Alex rubbed Owen's back. "Twice," he answered proudly.

"Well, if you can't keep it in your pants, keep it in the family, right?" Cameron asked cheekily. Owen's face shot up wide-eyed. "Tell me, Owen, did you make him cry Uncle?"

Alex shook his head. "Well, why go across town when you can go across the hall, right?"

"Stop!" Owen exclaimed, red-faced with embarrassment. "New rule. No incest jokes if you," he pointed at Cameron on the screen, "want me to do this interview," he pointed at Alex, "or if you ever want me to make your rooster crow or my bull to moo for you."

Cameron thought for a second. "Do bulls moo?"

"His does." Alex winked at Cameron.

Cameron covered his mouth to hide his laughter. "Maybe we should get started." He cleared his throat. "What I'm envisioning is you on camera talking to Alex, and I don't want to hide anything about your relationship with him. This entire thing needs to be completely transparent. It can't be only Alex's story. It also has to be Owen's introduction to the world."

"My introduction?" Puzzled, Owen looked at Alex, then back at Cameron. "What do you mean by my introduction? I thought this was all about Alex."

"When this thing goes out, your name is going to be all over it," Alex answered. "People are going to wonder who you are."

Cameron added, "They are going to pick you apart and try to destroy you." He smiled sympathetically. "It'll get easier after your second interview. I already know who it should be."

"Wait." Owen looked at Alex, then Cameron, in surprise. "This isn't a one-and-done?"

Alex pulled Owen closer. "Cameron, we didn't discuss a second interview."

"Where did you think this was going?" Cameron asked bluntly. "You said this was what you studied to do. This isn't only an opportunity for Alex to tell his story, it's an opportunity to get your name out there. When Aunt Lexi finds out, she's—"

Alex cut him off. "Wait. Lexi doesn't know about this?"

"Lexi?" Owen tried to remember how he knew that name. "Who is Lexi again?"

Cameron grinned. "She's my aunt. She's also the one who is going to tear Alex another asshole before she hugs him to death and then fawns over you."

"She's the one I was staying with after my unfortunate accident," Alex added. "I thought she hated me."

Cameron laughed. "She did, until she saw the real you in the hospital."

"She felt sorry for me," Alex sighed.

"She did," Cameron answered. "She also saw you were hurting more than physically." Cameron's eyes grew sympathetic. "Alex, you were broken and lost. She wasn't about to let you out of that hospital to self-destruct. Carlos even agreed that Aunt Lexi taking you in was in your best interest."

Alex chuffed. "That was so he knew where I was and away from you under Lexi's watchful eye."

"True." Cameron smiled with a wink. "I love how it drives him wild."

Owen held up a finger. "Excuse me, but can we get back to me?"

"Of course. I'm sending all the information now." Cameron grabbed his tablet. "Aunt Lexi is wanting to create a multimedia platform. News, entertainment, and more. We have ideas for shows, but not the people to do them." Cameron hit send on an email, then sat his tablet down. "This interview with Alex is going to be your audition. Despite what happens with her multimedia platform, if she likes or sees potential in your work, she's going to help you succeed."

Dumbfounded, Owen asked, "Why would she do that?"

"It's the type of person she is," Alex answered. "Taking in strays. Helping people when they are down. Lifting up those she can."

"Jordan Hudson can attest to that," Cameron confirmed. "She read one article of his and saw the potential in what he could do. Now he's a major name in writing and journalism and has more work than he can handle."

Owen sat frozen, his mind racing. "What if I fuck it up?"

"You won't," Alex reassured him, pulling him close. "You've got this."

Cameron added, "You also have me and Jordan as cheat sheets. We're going to make this a success." Cameron's crooked smile made Alex suspicious and Owen uneasy. "Are you two ready for my vision? It's not set in stone, and I want your input into it."

"Let's hear it," Owen answered nervously.

Cameron grabbed his tablet and read from it. "The interview is going to start off with Owen introducing himself, telling people why he agreed to do this interview, and whatever else." He winked. "When you open the file, you'll see it really does say whatever else."

"Cameron, hurry up please," Alex grumbled.

Cameron made a face at the camera. "Fine. Then it will be you two sitting across from each other doing the interview. No holds barred questions. I've sent some that I'd like you to work in from my time with Alex. Then fade to black." Cameron put his tablet down. "What do you think?"

"We're missing something," Owen said in thought. Cameron and Alex looked at him. "I need to interview you, too," he said to Cameron, then thought for a second. "And myself." He sucked his bottom lip. "Then we need to address our feelings to one another."

Cameron picked up his tablet. "I can fly to you sometime this week and I can stay until it's time for us to go to Mark and Hunter's wedding." He looked up from his tablet. "We can fly out together."

"I'm not going to that," Alex said regretfully. "No one there will want me there."

Cameron sat the tablet down and held up an invitation. "Hunter personally invited you. That means he does. I want you there. So there's two people."

"We really can't go anywhere too far," Owen explained. "We sort of put the town on notice and we still haven't finished dealing with his mother and sister yet."

Cameron sat the invitation down. "Just think about it, okay?" Alex nodded. "Okay, now I need to talk to Owen alone. Alex, why don't you go lift something heavy or take a thirst trap picture of yourself for about five minutes."

"I'll go check on the police officer outside; see if they need anything." Alex patted Owen's knee, then gave him a kiss on the cheek. "I'll wait outside until you're done."

When Alex left, Cameron asked, "Should I ask why there is a police officer outside your home?"

"Protection," Owen answered bluntly. "Last night we were refused service at a restaurant because of the lies his mother and sister spread. After Alex made a scene, I made a bigger one. I publicly announced we weren't going to continue to allow people who treat us like shit to rent from us." Owen couldn't help the slight upward curl of his lips. "We own the majority of the rental properties in the town. Houses, retail, apartments, the works, thanks to Terry."

Cameron raised an eyebrow. "Why didn't you do that before?"

"I didn't have Alex," Owen answered. He could feel the emotional pain stirring in his gut. "When Terry died, I didn't have anyone. I lost contact with my college friends when I had to take care of Terry. He passed, and I barely got a chance to grieve when those harpies tried to sink their claws in me and turned the town against me because they want this place." Hugging himself, Owen averted his eyes. "I'm scared of what's going to happen when they get out."

Gently, Cameron said, "You've got us now, Owen. You're now part of a wild, crazy, loving family that will do anything for you." Cameron cracked a smile. "Of course, we're not family like you and Alex are."

"You had to ruin it?" Owen laughed, feeling the sense of dread get pushed away. "Thanks. I needed that."

Cameron smiled softly into the camera. "You're welcome. Now let's get back to work." He picked up his tablet. "That right there needs to be in the interview. I know it's triggering, but you need to explain your unique relationship and the issues with Alex's family." He tapped on the tablet screen, sat it down, then gave Owen a confused look. "It feels like there's something more behind it all. Is there something you're not telling me?"

"They were blackmailing Terry by accusing him of inappropriate behavior with us." Owen thought about it. "Danielle all but admitted to killing her husband. They bounced around from house to house all over town because they couldn't or wouldn't pay rent. Once Krystal married her first husband, Danielle left Alex to fend for himself."

Cameron tapped his finger on the desk. "Why that place, though? From what you've said, you've got properties all over town. What is so special about your place in particular?"

"I have it," Owen answered with a shrug.

Cameron shook his head. "No. That might be part of it, but not all of it." He picked his tablet up and typed Owen's address into it. "Did they ever try to sell the land without you knowing or anything like that?"

"Yeah, once," Owen responded. "They tried to sell it to some company to build a factory or housing, but I stopped them and they lost interest once they found out the land is split between four different counties. It's a tax nightmare."

Cameron flipped his tablet to show Owen his screen. "They don't want your house or your property. They only want people to think they want it." Owen looked at the search results. Various different fundraisers were listed, all a variation on helping Danielle and Krystal get their land back. "I wonder how much money they have stolen from people over the years." Cameron sat the tablet down. "I can't believe they'd be this evil to do something like that."

"Isn't that technically illegal?" Owen asked, his interest growing.

Cameron's face twisted in thought. "Technically, it would be considered fraud. I'll pass this on to our attorneys over here, see what they say." Cameron turned his head to the side at the pounding on a door. "Carlos! I told you! I'm in a meeting! Go take a cold shower!" Under his breath, he mumbled, "For the rest of your life, if you keep acting like this."

"Trouble in paradise?" Owen observed.

Cameron rolled his eyes. "For some reason, Carlos is jealous of Alex." He held up one finger then turned and shouted to the side, "I swear if you make one more sound, I won't let you see Billy for a week!"

"That seemed to work," Owen laughed. "Who is Billy?"

Cameron smiled. "Billy is Jordan's boyfriend, and Carlos's best friend." Cameron thought for a moment. "Billy is like walking sunshine. You can't help but get wrapped up in his silliness." He put up a finger. "He's a snuggler and can't sleep unless he's snuggled up against someone. If you have to stay with him somewhere and Jordan isn't there, you'll wake up tangled in him."

"That seems oddly cute and creepy," Owen said, raising an eyebrow.

Cameron laughed. "He doesn't do that with strangers and we all know to expect it now." He chuckled. "He and Jordan once crashed at my Aunt Lexi's place after a party. Billy got up to get some water and couldn't find his way back to the room they were staying in." Cameron's chest shook with laughter. "He did find Aunt Lexi sleeping in her bed. Did I mention Billy sleeps in the nude?"

"Oh, no. What happened?" Owen asked, wide-eyed.

Cameron shook his head in amusement. "She cuddled him back, but before he woke up, she put on her lipstick and covered his body in kisses. Then she put a bottle of lube on the nightstand next to a strap-on. Then she woke him, asking if he still respected her." He let out a hearty laugh. "Billy shrieked so loud that

he woke up me and Carlos up across the hall. I opened the door to see Billy running naked out of her room covered in lipstick crying out for Jordan."

"I think I like your Aunt Lexi already." Owen laughed.

Cameron nodded. "I am lucky to have her in my life. We all are."

"I think I'd like to interview her next if we continue to do this," Owen said, feeling more relaxed about the possible future.

Cameron winked. "Who do you think I wanted your second interview to be?"

# ALEX AND CAMERON

"**WHAT DID YOU** say to Owen that has him grinning ear to ear now?" Alex asked, settling down on the couch.

Cameron looked at him with innocence. "I told him he was part of the family now, but not to expect to fuck any of the rest of us because we don't play like that off camera."

"Cameron," Alex groaned. "Be serious."

Cameron thought for a second. "Remember when I was all serious and broody all the time? Why in the world did you put up with me like that?"

"I slept with every man I could behind your back and you believed me when I said they were auditioning for my fan content," Alex answered bluntly. "Honestly, I don't know how we lasted as long as we did. We hated being with each other."

Cameron nodded. "Yeah, I think we had this dream of being some sort of power couple." Cameron cocked his head. "You've changed too. You're not an asshole anymore."

"I am, but to the appropriate people." Alex glanced at the front door. He smiled, knowing Owen was on the other side, waiting for him. "We're not the same people we were when we were together. We're actually happy."

"Speaking of which," Cameron peered intently into the camera, "how are you? Really?"

Alex worked his jaw in thought. "I'm happy. I know I have a lot of decisions to make, and I'm going to have to talk about things I don't want to talk about in order to do this for Owen. The thing is, though, I'm happy. I haven't been that in a long while."

"Do me a favor. If you need to talk, call me. Day or night." Cameron's face turned sympathetic. "I meant what I said to Owen about being part of this family. We're all here for you."

Off camera, Carlos shouted through the door, "Are you done yet?"

"One minute." Cameron smiled sweetly. Turning his head, he shouted back, "What did I tell you? Do it again and you won't get to see Billy for a week!"

Alex laughed. "Wow. What a punishment."

"It really is," Cameron huffed. "For me. At least if he's with Billy, Jordan can deal with their silliness." He shook his head. "Last week they got into a water gun fight … in a store. Actually, it started in the parking lot and ended up in a store."

Unable to contain his laughter, Alex asked, "How much trouble did they get into?"

"None," Cameron answered, wide-eyed. "Somehow, they enlisted the store manager and a bunch of random people. I still can't believe they got that seventy-year-old grandmother involved. She was hurling water balloons like a pro."

Alex fell back in laughter. "That was on the news! I remember that! It turned into a major water fight that filled the parking lot! That was because of them?!"

"Anyways," Cameron sighed, "I've forbidden any fights that aren't water-based after I saw the look in Carlos's eyes when Billy made cupcakes." Cameron shuddered at the memory. "I could see how badly he wanted to smash one of those cupcakes in Billy's face."

Alex wiped the tears of laughter from his eyes. "Good idea." Calmer, he said, "I need to make amends with them, too."

"We'll start small. With Jordan. Then we'll work our way through the group." Cameron gave him a sympathetic look. "Be the person you are right now with me and they'll listen. They may not forgive, but at least you'll have made the effort. That's all you can do."

Alex grew serious. "Have you and Carlos talked about having children?"

"I'm not adopting you," Cameron quickly shot out.

Alex shook his head. "I'm being serious."

"So am I." Cameron put his hands down on the desk. "We haven't talked about that yet, but I don't know if I want kids. I guess I'll find out if I do if and when Carlos and I have that talk. Why? Do you want kids?"

Alex shook his head affirmatively. "I do. I didn't realize I did until Owen and I talked about it."

"You love him. Like you really love him." Cameron put a hand over his heart. "Okay, now you have to go to the wedding because you know Hunter is going to be upset and hurt if he doesn't get to meet Owen."

Alex chewed the inside of his lip. "I'll think about it. We have so much going on here."

"I know." Cameron cleared his throat and did his best Lexi impression, "Get your shit together."

Alex flipped him off. "Fuck you." He bounced his eyes back and forth. "I may need your help with that, too. We're meeting with Owen's attorney tomorrow. He's filed so many official complaints about police harassment and it continued. Then there's Police Chief Anders. He doesn't sit right with me."

"Well, we figured out that your mom didn't want the house. She wanted the drama of wanting the land." Cameron thought out loud. "The cops that were harassing Owen, do they have any connections to your mother?"

"Cop. Singular," Alex corrected. "He's my brother-in-law. I found out after telling the bastard to get off our property."

Cameron thought for a moment. "Huh. What about the police chief? Could he be dating your mother?"

"He's still alive, so doubtful." Alex closed his eyes. "I don't know how he's connected to my mother at all."

Cameron tapped his fingers on his desk. "Or the lawyer. Let me have Lexi's people do some research and I'll get back to you, but it does sound like it's time to get a new attorney."

"Agreed." Guilt seeped into Alex. "I feel so bad that he's been going through all this alone. Last night

126

was the first time he's slept through the entire night peacefully since my uncle died."

Cameron's smile faltered. "Send me all the names of the players involved. I'll have Aunt Lexi's people look into it. In the meantime, get ready for this interview. I don't want him to pull any punches. I want him to ask the tough questions, even the triggering ones."

"I do too." Alex hugged himself. "Thank you for all your help, Cameron. It really means a lot to me and to Owen. I'll get you those names in a bit and I'm sorry that this is causing you to fight with Carlos."

Cameron snorted. "When are we not fighting? We really like making up, though. Oh, and you're welcome. Text me if you need me."

*We really have changed.* Alex picked up the phone and sent Cameron his mother's, sister's, and brother-in-law's name. Stepping outside, he smiled at Owen. "Do you know the police chief's full name? And what is your attorney's name?"

"It's Police Chief Joseph Anders and my attorney's name is Stephen Qualey." Owen watched him type the names into the phone. "Why?"

Putting his phone up, he took Owen in his arms. "Cameron is going to have Lexi's people look into them. Things don't seem right." Returning the embrace, Owen rested his head against Alex's chest. "I'm sorry I wasn't here for you. I should have been."

"We should have been honest with you," Owen said into his chest. "Let's stop talking about what we should have done and start talking about what we should do."

Alex's chest rumbled with laughter. "Like how you should get your ass in there and make your man something to eat."

"Excuse me?" Owen looked up at him. "Who said you were my man?"

Owen let out a shriek of surprise when Alex dipped him. He kissed Owen. "You know I've always been and will be your man." Righting Owen, he patted him on the ass. "Now get to cooking. That I honestly can't do."

"We're going to talk about your sudden toxic top tendencies." Owen glowered at him, stepping inside.

Alex pinched Owen's ass, causing him to yelp. "You know I'm verse, right?"

"Really?" Owen turned around and looked Alex up and down. "Good to know."

Alex grinned. "What are you thinking?"

"How sexy you'll look tied up with a ball gag in your mouth, nipple clamps, and a vibrating butt plug up your ass while I sound you." Owen erupted into laughter at the horror on Alex's face. "Don't worry, I was kidding about everything but tying you up." He winked. "Trust me enough to be at my mercy?"

Alex pulled him back into a hug. "Always."

# 19

# YOU STARTED IT

**O**WEN PULLED **ALEX'S** arms tighter around him. *I want to hate you, but I can't.* He settled back against Alex. *You should hate me, but you don't.*

"What's going on in that head of yours?" Alex whispered in his ear.

"Nothing," Owen lied.

Alex grazed his teeth across the back of Owen's neck. "Liar."

"Stop," Owen reprimanded with a shudder. "It's too late for your rooster to crow."

Alex's hand found its way to grope Owen's hard cock through his underwear. "Really? Because your bull is mooing."

"We really need to find out what sound a bull makes," Owen moaned.

Running his tongue along Owen's neck, Alex growled, "I know one way to find out." Alex pressed his arousal into Owen. "It'll help you fall asleep."

"Sex doesn't fix everything." Owen took Alex's hand off his crotch and pushed it into his underwear. "My cock is in there."

Alex stroked him. "I'm sorry. I guess I forgot where it was since it has been so long."

"If you're not up for it, I can grab my toy out of the nightstand," Owen teased.

Alex held him tighter. "Tonight I'm your toy and you're the box I come in."

"I am the original packaging you came in." Owen burst out in laughter. He rolled to face Alex. "Can we not do bad porn lines in bed?"

Alex pressed his lips to Owen's. "As long as we get to do porn things in and out of bed."

"Absolutely." Owen deepened the kiss.

Owned press forward, pushing Alex onto his back. They kissed clumsily, tangling their bodies in the sheets. Owen straddled Alex's waist, bunching up the sheets with his knees. Alex rolled them so he was on top, wrapping their bodies tightly in the sheets.

"Owen," Alex grunted, struggling to move. "We're wrapped tighter than a burrito."

Owen laughed, squirming against Alex's body with his nose pressed into Alex's face. "I can't move."

"Hold still." Alex tightened his grip around Owen, then rolled them so he was on top. "Better. Now get off me."

Owen ground his hips into Alex. "What if I don't want to?"

"Keep that up and you're going to make me cum." Alex tried shifting Owen off him and failed. "Then you're not getting my dick in you."

Owen straightened his legs, then rolled off Alex. "Fine." He tossed the sheets off of them, then shucked his underwear. Glancing at Alex, he asked, "Why aren't you naked yet?"

"Aren't we a horny little rabbit?" Alex took off his underwear and tossed them to the side. "Now where were we?"

Owen straddled Alex's hips, "Here."

Owen leaned down and kissed him. Alex's arms came around to hold him. He blindly reached over to the nightstand for the lube, knocking Alex's phone to the floor. With lube in hand, he sat up and looked down at Alex.

"Close your eyes," he ordered, before reaching over and turning on the lamp.

Alex winced at the sudden brightness. "Warn a guy."

"Next time, listen," Owen admonished, reaching behind himself to slip two lubed fingers into his hole. "I want to watch your face while I ride you." Leaning over Alex, Owen put a hand on Alex's muscular chest to steady himself. "Fuck, I need you in me."

"I need to be in you," Alex moaned, running his hands over Owen's body. Alex lurched up to try to capture Owen's mouth, but Owen evaded him. "Fucker."

Owen pulled his fingers out to grab Alex's cock. Stroking Alex's dick, he teased, "I said I wanted to watch your face, asshole."

Owen positioned Alex behind him. He took in a deep breath and let it out slowly as he lowered himself onto Alex's cock. His body burned hot, and he was vaguely aware of Alex's steading hands on his

body while Alex's dick slipped up into him, filling Owen's emptiness.

"When did your dick get so big?" Owen asked, resting on Alex's groin to allow himself to adjust. He rolled his body, starting with his neck, then traveling down his body. "Fuck, it feels good."

Alex ran his hands along Owen's thighs. "Breathe and relax."

"I know how to bottom you cock waffle." Owen raked his nails down Alex's chest. "It feels good to have you in me." He lightly pounded his fist into Alex's chest. "Fuck!"

Alex ran his hand up along Owen's side. "It feels good to be in you, but it's taking everything I have to hold still."

"Yeah?" Owen's hand lazily ran up Alex's chest, along his neck, over his chin to push two fingers into Alex's mouth. Alex ran his tongue over Owen's fingers as he sucked on them. "Good boy." Keeping his eyes locked with Alex's, he raised up slightly on his hips and lowered himself down. Owen moaned, "Fuck."

Owen pulled his fingers from Alex's mouth to brace himself on Alex's chest. He rose up and down, sliding Alex in and out of him. Gripping Owen's hips, Alex urged him to move faster, but Owen kept up his slow, languid pace while clenching and unclenching, trying to coax Alex's orgasm from him.

"You're evil." Alex tightened his grip on Owen, raised his knees slightly, and braced his feet. "Evil doers must be punished." He held Owen in place and started thrusting rapidly up into Owen.

Digging his fingers into Alex's chest, Owen arched his back and tossed his head back. His right hand went to his cock. He moaned through clenched teeth, "Fuck."

"Yeah," Alex growled, pumping his cock in and out of Owen. "I'm fucking you and you're going to be the only one I'm fucking from now on." He moved his right hand from Owen's hip to his head. "Do you hear me? I'm yours and you're mine."

Pumping his cock furiously, Owen crushed his mouth to Alex's. He started bouncing back against Alex's bucks. Pulling back from the kiss, Owen gasped, "Alex."

"Owen," Alex panted. His hand left Owen's head to return to his hip. "I'm going to fucking explode into you."

Owen's voice trembled when he spoke. "I'm going to paint your chest." Owen's body began to shake. "I'm going to blow. I'm going to blow." Owen exploded. White streaks shot across Alex's stomach and chest. "Fuck! Fuck! Fuck!"

"Owen!" Alex exclaimed, gripping Owen's hips tighter. He pumped furiously up into Owen's tight confines. "Fuck!" He arched his hips up, nearly throwing Owen off him as his cock exploded in Owen. He pulled Owen down on his hips as he pushed up. "Take it, baby! Take it!"

Alex's body shook with the force of his orgasm. He grabbed Owen by the head and pulled him back down into a hungry kiss. Owen collapsed on top of him. Alex wrapped his arms around him and held him

tight. Their kisses grew softer and gentler until Owen pulled away and rested his head on Alex's shoulder.

After a few quiet moments, Owen asked, "Did you mean what you said?"

"Hhmm?" Alex asked, stroking Owen's back.

Owen circled his finger on Alex's chest. "About being the only one you fuck."

"Yeah," Alex answered with certainty.

Hesitantly, Owen asked, "What about," he paused to find the right wording, "your work?"

"I haven't worked in ages, and honestly I haven't missed it." Alex tightened his hold on Owen. "It was what I needed to do to survive, but now what I need to survive is you."

Owen playfully smacked Alex's chest. "Now you sound like you're in a rom-com." He kissed Alex. "That was really sweet, though." He smiled down at Alex. "We should get cleaned up and get some sleep."

"It wasn't my idea to get dirty." Alex wiggled, coating their chests even further with the evidence of their bliss.

Owen pushed himself away and off of Alex. "You started it by groping me." He got out of bed and offered his hand to Alex. "Come on. I'll wash your back if you wash mine."

"Make sure you don't drop the soap," Alex teased, taking his hand and getting out of bed. Standing chest to chest with Owen, he asked, "What about you?"

Tugging Alex along, Owen asked innocently, "What about me, what?"

"Owen," Alex warned, pulling Owen back into his arms. "What about you?"

Owen looked into his eyes. "Only you." He kissed Alex. "It's always been only you."

FROM THE CORNER of the gas station, Alex kept an eye on Owen at the pump, filling up his car. Chewing his lip, he pulled out his phone and called the only person he could think to talk to. *Please, Cameron, please, don't be a dick.* Alex prayed as the call connected.

"Good morning, Uncle Fucker," Cameron said gleefully over the phone.

Annoyed, Alex did his best to sound polite. "Good morning, Cameron."

"Hold on a second." The sound of Cameron moving about, then a door shutting, came over the phone. "Okay, I just needed some privacy. What's going on?"

Alex stared at Owen, leaning against his car, holding the pump to the gas tank. "Cameron, I need some advice. I made a decision last night and now I don't know what to do. It was the right decision for me. The thing is, I don't know what I'm going to do now."

"What did you decide?" Cameron asked, concerned.

Alex pointed to his phone when he saw Owen looking at him. "I decided to leave porn… or, rather, not go back."

"I can respect that decision. Can I ask why?" Cameron probed.

Alex felt guilty telling Cameron his answer. "Owen."

"Owen?" Cameron questioned. "Could you elaborate?"

Alex feared the truth would hurt Cameron, but he said it anyway. "I can see me building a life with Owen and I don't see porn being a part of the future I want to have with him."

"It was a future you saw with others?" Cameron asked with a hint of bitterness. "Don't answer that. That wasn't fair, considering I haven't pressured Carlos the way I pressured you to leave the industry." Cameron paused. "Speaking of…" Cameron's muffled yell came over the speaker. "Your ass better be cleaning up your room and not playing that stupid video game!" Back to Alex, he said, "Sorry. Jordan and I have a meeting with Aunt Lexi so Jordan is dropping Billy off to have a playdate with Carlos."

Alex laughed, "Playdate? What do they do on their playdates?"

"You know, boys' stuff like hit the gym, play video games, cook us dinner, and sometimes film content," Cameron answered casually. "Today I think they are going to film each other jerking off while wearing women's lingerie."

Shocked, Alex said, "I don't remember you being so cavalier when I did something similar."

"Let's just say Carlos has expanded my menu," Cameron responded slyly.

Alex laughed. "I see."

"Back to you," Cameron redirected. "You're leaving the industry. Great. I know you have money saved, and you found out you're part owner of a rental company, so you can't need advice about money. What do you need advice on?"

Alex let out a sigh of frustration. "What do I do? We went to the property management company, and it runs itself. Owen is hopefully going to be working as a journalist. What am I going to do? Sit at home and jerk myself raw?"

"You can do whatever you want," Cameron answered bluntly. "You can go back to school. Open your own business. Be Owen's production manager. You can sit at home and jerk yourself raw if you want." Cameron paused. "Hold on." Cameron's muffled shout came over the speaker. "No, you cannot sit at home all day jerking off!" Cameron returned to the phone. "Where was I? Oh, yeah. You don't have to decide right now, today, or tomorrow. You have time."

Alex held up a finger to Owen. "Thanks. That helped a lot. I better get going. Owen is scowling at me." Alex chewed his lower lip. "Cameron, if me calling and texting you is causing problems between you and Carlos—"

"It's not," Cameron cut him off. "Carlos is being a jealous jerk. He has nothing to worry about and needs to get over it." Mischief entered his voice. "Besides, fighting means we get to have makeup sex."

Alex groaned. "Bye, Cameron. I'm hanging up now."

"Bye, Uncle Fucker," Cameron singsonged.

Hanging up, Alex made his way to Owen's car. Hopping in the passenger's side, he felt more at ease. "We've returned my rental, gone to the property management company, so your piece of shit lawyer next?"

"That's correct." Owen started the car. "Who were you on the phone with?"

Alex fastened his seatbelt. "Cameron. He helped me get some perspective."

"Good." Owen pulled out onto the road. "I like him. I can't wait to meet him in person." Xavier's name came up on the car's digital display. "Why is he calling?" Owen answered the call. "Hey, Xavier, you're on speaker."

"Good." Xavier's voice was serious and full of concern. "I can't go into specifics right now, but Danielle and Krystal didn't show up to their arraignment, which was very inconvenient for the officers from California there to serve extradition papers." Xavier paused to take a breath. "Those boys from California raised some hell. Half the police force is in state custody, the other half, like me, are suspended pending a state police investigation."

Alex reached over and took Owen's hand. "What about my mom and sister? Why were they being extradited to California?"

"You," Xavier answered bluntly. "Someone tipped them off to investigate them and those dumb bitches— sorry, Alex."

Alex squeezed Owen's hand. "No need to apologize."

"They were posting on their social media and forgot to turn off the location services," Xavier explained.

"They posted on their very public accounts photos of them at the crime scene right before it happened."

Owen gave Alex's hand a squeeze. "Now all we need to do is find them."

"Then it's a matter of who gets them first," Xavier added. "I overheard something about launching a fraud investigation about some crowdfunding scheme."

Alex brought Owen's hand to his lips for a kiss. "What about the people in town?"

"News spread like wildfire." Amusement snuck into Xavier's voice. "They forgot how mad they are at you two and are furious at Danielle, Krystal, Anders, Stewie, and some attorney who helped them set it up. What is his name? It's a strange name… what was it?"

"Stephen Qualey," Owen answered.

"Yeah, that sounds right," Xavier confirmed. "How did you know?"

Owen carefully pulled into a parking lot and stopped. "Because that's the name of my attorney and he's being taken out of the building in handcuffs."

"That explains why none of those complaints were followed up on and nothing was done to stop the harassment." Alex gave Owen's hand a squeeze. "I guess we should go home then."

Owen shook his head in disbelief. "I can't believe it."

"Maybe I should drive." Alex got out of the car, went to Owen's side, and helped him out and into the passenger's seat. "Are you okay?" Alex asked, getting into the driver's seat.

Owen vibrated with anger, then let out a screech.

"Damn, warn a guy." Xavier's voice came over the car. "I'll meet you guys at your place just to give it a once over. Okay?"

Alex patted Owen's knee, then put the car in drive. "Thanks, Xavier. Can you also find out if they need to talk to us?"

"I'm sure they do, but I'll tell them you guys need to process everything before you come in." Xavier's voice sounded relieved. "Owen, it's over. All that hell. It's over."

Owen's eyes were red with tears. "Thanks, Xavier. We'll see you in a bit." When the call ended, Owen asked, "Cameron did this, didn't he?"

"Yeah, I think he did." Alex reached over and took Owen's trembling hand.

Looking out the window, Owen said, "I really like that guy."

# MORNING COFFEE

**O**WEN CAREFULLY UNRAVELED himself from a sleeping Alex. He took a moment to appreciate the tranquil expression on Alex's face. Alex shivered slightly, so he pulled the sheets up to cover Alex's exposed chest. He brushed a stray lock from Alex's forehead before heading to the bathroom to relieve himself.

He grabbed his phone off the nightstand on his way to the kitchen. Pouring himself a cup of coffee, he curled up on the couch, coffee in one hand, his cell phone with a blank message addressed to Cameron on the screen in the other. [Thank you.] He sent, then sat the phone down.

A moment later, his phone rang with Cameron's name on the screen. "Good morning," Owen answered. "I didn't expect you to be up this early."

"I'm not," Cameron yawned. "Go back to sleep, baby," he said to someone Owen assumed was Carlos. "Hold on, let me go to the other room so I don't wake snorezilla." There was a moment of silence and the soft shut of a door. "Now, good morning, and what are you thanking me for at this ungodly hour?"

Owen laughed softly. "Isn't it like seven in the morning where you're at?"

"Your point being?" Cameron asked, smacking his dry lips. "I need tea. Hold on. I'm putting you on speaker." Owen heard the opening and closing of cabinets, then the whirl of a machine starting. "Anyways, why are you thanking me?"

Owen hugged his knees to his chest. "Everything. For taking care of Alex, being there for him, for loving him, for this interview opportunity, for getting us the equipment and tipping off the cops on his mom and sister…"

"I didn't tip off the police," Cameron said, confused. "When I called them yesterday, they told me someone else had already emailed them the tip along with links to Alex's mom's and sister's social media posts putting them at the scene of the crime last week."

Owen sat baffled on the couch. "Then who did?"

"Did you seriously get out of bed with me to talk to that asshole?" Carlos's grumpy voice came over the phone.

Cameron snapped back, "I'm talking to Owen and we're trying to figure out who tipped off the police about Alex's mom and sister."

"I should let you go," Owen stammered out.

Cameron retorted angrily, "No, Carlos should stop being a jealous prick and go back to bed."

"Fine," Carlos shot back angrily. "Then I won't tell you who emailed the cops."

Cameron's voice grew sharp. "Carlos, what do you know?"

"Hey! Let go of my dick! You know that's my money maker!" Carlos shouted.

Owen chuckled to himself. "Please, don't turn him into a eunuch with me on the phone."

"I won't. Then I'd have to top all the time." Cameron's voice went sultry. "I will overlook his earlier comment and show him some appreciation if he answers."

Carlos moaned, "Oh, Chipmunk."

"Did he just call you Chipmunk?" Owen chuckled. "Why did he call you Chipmunk?"

Carlos answered in a husky voice, "Because he wants my nut between his cheeks. Both sets."

"You really need to stop telling people that," Cameron groaned in embarrassment.

Carlos growled, "I like how you punish me after, like what you did that night when—"

"Speakerphone!" Owen called out frantically. "Carlos, please, tell us who tipped off the cops so Cameron can reward you without me on the phone."

Carlos huffed, "Fine. It's better when he's mad at me, though."

"Carlos!" Cameron snapped.

Carlos sighed, "It was Lexi. She and I were talking while you were in the hospital room with Alex. It was right after he tried calling his mom and she never answered. We were worried that something happened to her, so she hired Caleb to do a little digging. Lexi turned everything he found over to the investigators last week."

"Thank you, Carlos," Cameron said merrily. "You can go back to bed now."

Carlos whined, "You woke him up. At least give him a kiss good morning. It's been two weeks."

"Stop being a jealous asshole, and maybe I'll give you a little," Cameron scolded. "Now, go back to bed."

Owen blushed. "Two weeks? I've seen your man. How have you resisted him for two weeks?"

"Cold showers mostly," Cameron groaned. "Unfortunately, withholding sex is the only way to really punish him. The problem is that it's also a punishment for me."

Owen sipped his coffee. "What did he do?"

"He's been a jerk about Alex." Cameron sighed. "He doesn't get it. Yes, Alex did me wrong. If he hadn't, I wouldn't have met Carlos and I wouldn't be making a name for myself."

Owen smiled. "And he wouldn't be here with me now."

"Exactly. You owe me for breaking up with him," Cameron said conspiratorially. "Owen, I need your help to convince Alex to go to Mark's and Hunter's wedding."

Owen glanced back toward the bedroom and a groggy, naked Alex swaying down the hall, scratching his balls. "Fuck convincing him. I'm going to tell him."

"Good morning, babe," Alex yawned, scratching his chest.

Owen put Cameron on speaker. "Which babe are you saying good morning to?"

"Good morning, Alex," Cameron called out over the phone. "Your uncle boyfriend doesn't understand time zones."

Alex shook his head. "Too early for this." He headed to the kitchen. "Coffee."

"Alex, we're going to the wedding," Owen announced.

Alex took a healthy sip of his coffee. "Whose wedding?"

"Mark's and Hunter's," Cameron answered.

Alex took a seat beside Owen and snuggled up next to him. "I'm not awake enough to have this argument."

"It'll be good for me to meet everyone for the interview, and I need you for moral support." Owen slipped an arm around Alex. "Plus, if we don't go, I'm not plucking your rooster until I'm done being mad at you."

Alex kissed Owen on the cheek. "So five minutes from now?"

"Oh, yeah, well," Owen stumbled for words. "I'll get a cock cage, lock your rooster up while you're sleeping, mail Cameron the key and when he decides I'm no longer mad at you, he'll mail it back for me to unlock you."

Cameron laughed. "He's going to be mad for a very, very long time."

"I'll fly out, but I won't go to the wedding," Alex negotiated. "You can go to the wedding with Cameron and Carlos."

Owen nibbled on his ear. "Will you go with me to go buy a suit this week? Hhmm, maybe get one

for you for the court appearances we'll have to make." Owen purred in Alex's ear. "I bet you look super sexy in a suit."

"You're not playing fair," Alex said with a shudder. "Fine."

Cameron chimed in, "Since it sounds like you two are about to fornicate like bunnies and I haven't gotten any in two weeks, I'm hanging up. Bye, guys."

"Bye Cameron!" Alex and Owen called out together.

Setting his phone down, Owen shifted to let Alex rest on his chest. "You know you're walking around the house naked, right?"

"Yup, and you're wearing too many clothes." Alex relaxed back into Owen. "It sounds like you and Cameron are really getting along."

Owen stroked Alex's chest. "Yeah, I like him." He lightly tapped Alex's chest. "Oh, it wasn't Cameron who tipped off the cops. It was someone called Lexi. She hired some private investigator while you were in the hospital."

"Lexi, always stepping up to help, even when you don't know you need it." Alex sat up slightly to drink his coffee. "Why hasn't Cameron been getting any? Is Carlos doing a bunch of shoots?"

Owen traced the outline of Alex's nipple with his finger. "Carlos is being a jealous jerk over you. That's why you have to go to the wedding. You have to show Carlos you don't want Cameron, that you want me so Cameron can get laid."

"Wow. I have to go to the wedding so Cameron can get laid by his boyfriend?" Alex patted Owen's hand. "I'll think about it."

Owen tweaked Alex's nipple. "Think about how I'm going to reward you for going."

"Mm. You didn't mention there would be rewards," Alex growled, interlacing his fingers with Owen's and bringing Owen's hand to his mouth for a kiss. "Do we have time for me to get a preview?"

Owen grumbled, "I wish, but we've got to finish setting up the room and we've got to stop by the station to give our statements."

"I've got to put on clothes, don't I?" Alex whined.

Owen's chest shook with laughter. "Yes, you have to put on clothes." Alex started to get up, but Owen pulled him back down. "But not right now. I'm enjoying the view."

# CAMERON COMES TO TOWN

**A**NNOYED WITH THE back-and-forth Owen was doing with James on the phone, Alex snatched it from Owen's ear and put the call on speaker. "This is what we're doing," Alex snapped. "Anyone up to three months past due can get on a repayment program. Anyone over three months past due has to catch their balance up to three months to get on the program. End of story."

"Um, okay. Understood," James said timidly over the phone. "Anything else?"

"Yes," Alex continued gruffly, "until further notice, call me first and then Owen if it's an emergency. He has a special project he has to focus on."

"It would be best," Owen confirmed.

James was silent for a moment, then said, "Okay, and notifications will go out to the tenants this afternoon. You two have a good day."

"Look at you being mister boss man," Owen teased when the call ended. "I'm sorry. I should have had you on that call from the start."

Alex pulled Owen against him. "It's okay. You're used to doing it all alone, but you don't have to anymore." He kissed the top of Owen's head. "Now you can focus on what you're supposed to be doing, figuring out what you're going to say on camera."

"I know," Owen groaned. "When do you have to go pick up Cameron?"

Alex nuzzled Owen. "I should leave soon. Are you going to be okay on your own?"

"Yes, Daddy," Owen teased.

Alex growled in his ear, "I like it when you call me daddy."

"Gross." Owen pushed him away. "Go get Cameron while I still have the slightest desire to have sex with you."

Alex stood and looked around the spacious apartment they temporarily resided in. "Why did you stay in the cabin when you could have stayed in this apartment in the city?"

"Because your mom and sister would have moved into the cabin and I would have had more issues to deal with." Owen leaned back and stretched out on the couch. "This is the apartment Terry got me for school. It's where he stayed when the treatments were too much to go back home or his appointments ran late." Owen glanced around. "Three bedrooms. One for me. One for him. One for…"

Alex finished, "Me."

"Yeah," regret tinged Owen's voice. "I sometimes wonder what would have happened if we'd been able to bring you with us."

Putting a hand on the back of the sofa, Alex leaned down and kissed Owen. "I would have screwed things up somehow, being the young naïve kid I was." He kissed Owen again. "I needed to go through what I did so we could be together."

"The same." Owen smiled at him. "Now go get Cameron. I know what to ask now."

"Hello, Uncle Fucker," Cameron said cheekily as he slid into the passenger seat.

Alex gripped the steering wheel hard. "Could you not call me that in front of Owen?"

"I'll stop." Cameron slipped on the seat belt. "For him. I'm looking forward to meeting Owen. He seems like a great guy."

Alex pulled out into traffic. "He is." He smiled brightly. "He really is."

"You love him, don't you?" Cameron glanced over and saw Alex's huge smile. He playfully smacked Alex. "You do! You fucking love him!" He relaxed back in his seat. "Good for you."

Alex felt no shame in admitting it. "Yes, I do and, before you ask, no, I haven't looked to see if I can marry my uncle."

"I checked, you can because he's not blood-related," Cameron supplied gleefully. "When you're ready, of course. No pressure."

Alex sighed. "We just found each other again. We sort of slipped back into each other."

"I bet you did," Cameron teased.

Playfully annoyed, Alex said, "Anyways, with everything going on with my mom and sister." He paused. "Owen put his life and dreams on hold because of my family. It's time for Owen to live his life, to chase his dreams, and I want him to. Whether it includes me or not."

"I have a feeling his life and dreams include you," Cameron reassured him.

Alex stared straight ahead. "I hope you're right."

Alex nervously opened the apartment door. "Owen?" he called out when he didn't see Owen on the couch. "We're here." He grew nervous when no one answered. "Owen?"

"Is he not here?" Cameron asked, stepping into the apartment. "Nice place."

Alex's heart started racing. "Owen?!" he called out in a near panic. "Owen, where are you?"

"Taking a piss." Owen stepped out of their bedroom. A moment later, he found himself wrapped in Alex's arms. "Hey, strong man, you break me, you bought me."

Alex relaxed. "Sorry, I got scared for a second."

"I get it." Owen returned the hug. "I totally get it."

Cameron cleared his throat. "I get it, too."

"Cameron." Owen tried to pull away. "Alex, let me go." Alex squeezed him and then let him go. "Thank you."

Cameron extended his hand to Owen. "Owen, it is a pleasure to finally meet you in person."

"The same." Owen took his hand. "Thank you so much for everything."

Jokingly, Cameron said, "Thank you for not making me sleep in a cabin in the woods."

"Well, it was strongly suggested that we stay somewhere else until things cool down." Owen withdrew his hand. "I also didn't think you'd like sleeping on a couch."

Cameron gave Owen an incredulous look. "Oh, honey, Alex would have been sleeping on the couch. We would have shared a bed and made him wonder."

"We do want to film in the cabin though," Alex spoke up, coming up and slipping an arm around Owen's waist. "I set everything up yesterday."

Cameron nodded. "It'll give it a home feel. I like it." Cameron cocked his head at the two men in front of him. He smiled.

"What?" Owen asked self-consciously.

Cameron shook his head. "Nothing." He grabbed the handle of his luggage. "How about showing me where I'll be sleeping?"

# 23

# HATE ME NOW, LOVE ME LATER

**O**WEN SAT NERVOUSLY in his chair across from Cameron while Alex adjusted the lighting and tested their microphones. *We're doing this. We're really doing this.* Owen took in several deep breaths.

"Owen, relax." Cameron's voice snapped him out of his thoughts. "We're just doing a test shoot to get light and volume levels." He placed a hand on Owen's bouncing knee. "You're going to do great."

With panic-stricken eyes, Owen asked, "Then why did you do my hair and makeup?"

"So we can get the right lighting," Alex answered. "I'm not going to be here for these parts, so I have to get the lighting right before I leave."

Owen took several more deep breaths. "Okay," he said anxiously.

"Owen," Cameron said in a gentle, yet commanding, voice. "Look at me." Owen turned his fear-stricken eyes on Cameron. "I want you to look at me the entire time, not the cameras. They aren't here.

We're just two versatile bottoms talking shit about our mutual ex."

Alex cried out, "Hey!" He focused on Cameron. "When did you become verse?"

"I always was, asshole." Cameron stood and pulled out his cell. "Time to call an expert. I'll be right back."

When Cameron left the room, Owen asked, "How do you do it?" When Alex looked at him with confusion, he clarified, "Forget that the cameras are there."

"I just do." Alex thought for a moment. "I guess in my head the camera is just another person that is either watching or I'm sharing myself with."

Cameron stuck his head back in. "Alex, can I see you for a moment?"

*I'm fucking this up*, Owen told himself when Alex left the room. *Cameron is probably telling Alex they need to replace me.*

"Okay, change of plans," Cameron announced, coming back in. "We're going to interview each other with the cameras off but with the lighting and wearing our mics to give you the feel."

Alex followed, going to the cameras. "I'm turning the cameras off, then heading out."

"I thought you were going to replace me," Owen admitted with a sigh of relief.

Cameron put a comforting hand on Owen's knee. "This doesn't work without you." He winked at Owen. "Plus, I didn't lend you clothes, or do your hair and makeup for nothing." He turned to look at Alex. "If you're done, you can go off and do whatever. We'll text when we're done."

"Bossy bottoms," Alex muttered jokingly.

Cameron quipped back, "Someone has to remind you tops that you're nothing more than a pole."

"This pole is only for this man's hole." Alex pecked Owen on the lips, careful not to ruin his makeup. "Do you need anything while I'm out?"

Owen shook his head, a little more at ease because of the banter. "I'm good. Thank you."

"I'll text you my coffee order when we summon you back," Cameron chimed in. He blew Alex a kiss. "Bye now."

Alex caught the imaginary heart, then handed it back to Cameron. "Sorry, I only accept kisses as payment from Owen."

"I'll pay for his later. Now go so we can see how badly I do." Owen rubbed his palms up and down his legs.

Alex knelt down. Putting his hands on top of Owen's, he looked him in the eyes. "Forget the lights and cameras. It's only you and Cameron talking about your favorite subject: me."

"Asshole." Owen laughed, feeling more at ease. "Thank you."

Cameron cleared his throat. "If this romantic movie scene is over, I'd like to get started."

"Be honest. Be real. No sugar coating. The good with the bad." Giving Owen's hands a squeeze, Alex stood. "Okay?"

Owen nodded. "Okay."

Cameron pointed to the door. "Go. Now. I'll take care of him. Promise."

"You better." Alex winked at Owen, then turned to face Cameron. "He's my favorite uncle."

Alex rushed out when Owen shouted, "Go!"

"Great, now I need to fix your hair and makeup." Cameron pulled out his kit and started fixing the slight imperfections. "Perfect." He put his kit aside and returned to his seat. "Ready?"

"So, how do we start?" Owen asked, looking around.

Cameron spoke soothingly. "The questions are on the screens behind us. Use the clicker when you're ready for the next question," Cameron explained. "The screen behind me has your questions for me, and the screen behind you has the questions I have for you." He saw terror slinking its way across Owen's face. "Owen, I'm going to be pissed if you make me ruin your hair and makeup by me coming over there and slapping you to get you out of your head." Cameron put bite in his voice. "Get your shit together."

"I'm sorry." Owen exhaled the panicked breath he was holding. "It's that so much is riding on this, and I don't want to let Alex or you down."

Cameron knew that pressure and self-doubt. "Owen, forget all that. This is just a rehearsal. I'm going to ask you questions, you're going to ask me questions. Pretend we're having a conversation and don't be afraid to ad-lib questions, okay?"

"Okay," Owen said, a bit more relaxed.

Cameron smiled. "Mentally count to ten, then start."

"Okay." Owen closed his eyes. *Get your shit together.* He opened his eyes and counted down in his head. "I'm Cameron—fuck!"

Cameron laughed, "I'm Cameron, and that's not my last name."

"I'm sorry. I'm already screwing up," Owen said, flustered.

Sympathetically, Cameron said, "Do you think everyone does it right on the first try? Get out of your head and get out here with me. Reset, then start again. We're not leaving until we've gone through this at least once."

"The police don't want us here after dark since they are shorthanded," Owen blurted out. "They don't have the staff to keep someone out here for us."

Cameron smirked. "Then you better get it right before nightfall, huh?"

"You're an ass." Owen closed his eyes and began taking deep, centering breaths. *Get your shit together. You can do this. You did this in school,* he reassured himself. "Ready." He mentally counted down to ten while summoning his courage.

Smiling, Owen opened his eyes and faced the camera he was supposed to for his opening. "Hello, I'm Owen Sparks and I'm here with Cameron Matthews. We're here to explain why we chose to do this project. We want to be completely transparent about our ties to the subject of this project. This project is about Alex Sparks. Both Cameron and I have unique relationships with Alex Sparks."

Owen paused to breathe. "I met Alex when I was sixteen, when his uncle took me in. He was my first boyfriend and I'm currently in a relationship with him now."

"I was engaged to Alex," Cameron continued. "I didn't have direct communication with Alex after our engagement ended until I received a call from the

hospital that he was involved in a hit-and-run accident. He recovered at my aunt's house, Lexi Luscious."

Owen cut in, speaking with sincerity. "We're not doing this to try and redeem Alex or punish him. We are here to let Alex tell his story, ask uncomfortable questions about his actions, and challenge his justifications for what he did."

"And each other." Cameron turned to Owen. "Which is why, Owen, I am going to ask you why you are really doing this and to elaborate about your history with Alex."

Owen was thrown off by the random question but recovered quickly. He looked at Cameron and spoke from the heart. "I'm doing this because I love Alex and he loves me. He's doing this, and asked me to do this, because he wants me to know everything about our time apart. That's why he gave me carte blanche to ask whatever I want."

Owen shifted uncomfortably. "My relationship with Alex is complicated." He felt the pain with his words as he relived the memory. "At sixteen, my father was no longer able to take care of me. Terry, Alex's uncle, took me in. The situation was supposed to be temporary. I was supposed to move back in with my dad when he…" Owen trembled with pain. "Let's say I haven't seen my father since."

"I'm sorry. I didn't know." Cameron stood. "You don't have to do this."

Owen continued, with tears streaking down his cheeks. "I met Alex the day I moved in. He was a scrawny stick boy then." Wiping away his tears, he laughed. "I remember thinking how much I wanted

to kiss him, and two years later, I did." Owen took a moment to gather himself. "Terry hoped we'd be friends, but we became each other's everything for the next two years."

Owen's Adam's apple bobbed as he dry swallowed. "That's why it hurt so much to keep his family's secrets from him." He wiped his eyes. "His uncle was sick and his mother was, well, that's his story." He took in a deep breath and exhaled. "That's why Terry and I did what we did and couldn't tell Owen."

"What did you guys do?" Cameron asked quietly.

Owen looked up and let out a humorless laugh. "We're really going to go on record with this." He looked at the camera with red-rimmed eyes. "Terry needed to ensure he had someone he could trust for his care and that no one unraveled what he did for Alex and me." He shrugged. "Part of that was that I secretly married Terry without Alex knowing."

"How did Alex take it?" Cameron leaned forward, offering a box of tissues.

Owen took a tissue and dabbed at his eyes. "The plan was for Terry to get me settled in my condo, go for his treatment, then grab Alex and bring him up the next day." Owen shook his head. "The treatment didn't go well, and I had to take care of Terry for the next three weeks. When Terry went back, he couldn't find Alex, and his phone was dead."

"Take your time," Cameron said softly, handing him a water bottle.

Owen took a swig, then wiped his mouth with the back of his hand. "No one would tell us if they saw him, not even his mom and sister. I can still see the

cruel delight on their faces when they called us perverts and freaks."

Owen wiped his eyes. "The next time I saw him was at Terry's funeral, after his family filled his head with lies." Owen shook his head. "Things were said. Hurtful things. By both of us." Owen's breath hitched. "I didn't see him again until he showed up on our doorstep two years later." Owen sighed. "I tried to hate him. I wanted to."

"You couldn't, though, could you?" Cameron interjected.

Owen shook his head. "No. I saw how broken, angry, and hurt he was—no, is—despite his tough veneer. I couldn't deny that I had a hand in making him that way. I was surprised that he didn't hate me once he knew everything." Owen wiped at his eyes. "That's why I'm doing this. For us."

"What do you mean for us?" Cameron prodded.

"Alex isn't doing this for forgiveness or redemption." Owen chewed his lower lip. "He's doing this so I can break down his walls and he can come clean to me about all the things he's done. He wants people to know he regrets what he did and that he's sorry. He wants me and the world to know that he's no longer that person."

Cameron sat up straight. "You don't think he wants forgiveness from those he wronged?"

"He can want it, but he knows that he can't expect forgiveness from everyone." Owen took a sip of water. "Now that I've bared my soul, why have you agreed to do this project?"

Cameron smirked. "As pretty much everyone knows, Alex was my fiancé, and we had a very public and viral break up. We dated for a year. I really can't say that I loved him like I should have for a boyfriend. In fact, I know I can't. I was more interested in the prestige of saying I was dating Alex Sparks."

Cameron looked at Owen earnestly. "Alex didn't love me that way, either. We were only going through the motions. He cheated on me. Brought me out when he needed to at events, but in the end we weren't meant for a happily ever after with each other. I knew his heart didn't belong to me. It was after our recent conversations over the past couple of days that I realized it always belonged to you."

Cameron sighed. "Like you, I tried to hate him. I really wanted to hate him. Then I saw how far he fell after. All of his so-called friends abandoned him. His fans were turning against him and I met the love of my life, Carlos." He cocked his head and glared at the camera. "There, Latin Lover. I admitted it. You're the love of my life."

He returned his attention to Owen and hugged himself. "I felt sorry for him. Then he got hit by that car." Cameron's voice saddened. "Of all people for him to wake up to, it was his ex, his ex's current boyfriend, and his ex's aunt. Then his family wouldn't take his calls, and never returned his texts or calls."

Cameron began to get choked up. "Like you, I saw how broken, hurt, and angry he was. He was hotel hopping and couch surfing. He was spiraling down, and he needed someone to be his friend." He smiled warmly at Owen. "I'm glad he found you again. You're

good for him. He's been more of his true self since he's been back with you."

He brushed away a tear. "As to why I'm doing this, well, I think most people can agree I was the one person Alex wronged the most. I'm hoping that if people see that I can forgive him, then maybe they can, too." Cameron mentally counted to ten. "That was fantastic!"

"I hope I can remember all of that when we actually do film." Owen dried his tears. "Can we take a break? I'm mentally drained. You can fix my makeup and stuff and then we'll shoot it for real."

Cameron looked at him guiltily. "No need. The cameras were recording the whole time."

"What?!" Owen's head darted from camera to camera. "I can't believe you did that!"

Cameron shrugged. "It was Jordan's idea. It's how he got used to being in front of the camera. He told them not to let him know when they were filming. He still hates being on camera, but now he's more comfortable."

"I don't know whether to hate you or love you right now." Owen stood. "I'll make us some tea and decide."

Cameron called after him, "You'll hate me now, but love me later!"

# 24

# WALKING AWAY

**A**LEX TURNED HIS phone off before pocketing it. He dreaded opening the door in front of him. What lay behind it, in handcuffs, chained to a table, was his mother. His mother, with her venomous distorted truth and her cruel scheming ways. He wanted answers that he doubted she would give him.

Opening the door, he stared into her heartless, angry eyes. "Hello, Mom."

"What do you want?" she spat out when Alex sat down.

*A mother that loved me,* Alex thought. As he sat down, he saw the answers she wouldn't give him in her twisted, gnarled face. She was a selfish, bitter woman, incapable of loving anyone other than herself. *I doubt she even loves Krystal. She was just a means for my mother to support herself.*

"Well?" Danielle snapped Alex out of his thoughts.

Alex studied her face, praying to find a glimmer, even a hint of love or remorse in her. He saw none.

"Are you here to gloat?" Danielle's cold-hearted voice echoed in the small room. "Or are you here to tell me what an awful person and mother I am?"

"No." Alex shook his head. His voice was calm, nearly emotionless. "You already know that."

Angered at Alex's tranquil demeanor, Danielle spat out, "What then?"

Alex felt the emotional chains she bound him in shatter. "I came to say goodbye."

"You've been nothing but a disappointment since you were born." Danielle tried to tie him up with her malicious barbs. "I should have smothered you when you were a child."

Alex looked at her with pity. Giving her a sad smile, he stood and said, "I'll see you at the trial." Walking away from her, Alex felt free.

"You're nothing more than a pathetic whore loser!" When Alex didn't react, Danielle shouted at his back. "You can go to Hell for all I care!"

Opening the door to the interrogation room, Alex turned to take one last look at his mother. "I spent my childhood in Hell, I don't plan on going back." He shut the door.

"You okay?" Xavier asked, placing a hand on Alex's shoulder.

Alex smiled, feeling genuine relief. "I am." He looked at Xavier. "Krystal still doesn't want to see me?"

"She declined to see you with some extremely colorful language," Xavier answered.

Alex pulled his phone out and turned it on. "It's not like we were really close. She was ten when I was born."

"Owen should be relieved you guys can go back home." Xavier led him to the front. "The town might hate you guys, but they hate Danielle, Krystal, Stewie, and Anders more."

Alex offered his hand to Xavier. "Thanks, but I think we'll be staying in the city for a while, and only coming back here to do our work. Too many bittersweet memories."

"I understand." Xavier took his offered hand. "If there's anything I can do for you, just let me know."

Alex's phone buzzed with a message. Taking it out and reading the message, he asked, "How about the name of a coffee shop that won't spit in my latte or poison our coffees?"

# 25

# ALEX COMES CLEAN

**S**TILL UNEASY IN front of the camera, Owen sat patiently while Cameron did his makeup. Alex busied himself doing his own with the strange calm he had returned with after secretly seeing his mother at the police station. Owen knew he should have been mad at Alex for not telling him he was going or taking him along, but he wasn't.

*"I needed to do it on my own," Alex explained, taking Owen in his arms. He studied Owen's face. "Have you been crying?"*

*Cameron called out from the couch, "Oh, yeah. I broke your uncle boyfriend. Sorry."*

*"Are you okay?" Alex asked, concerned and cradling Owen's cheek.*

*"I was already broken. He helped me see it so I could put myself back together," Owen said with a smile.*

*Alex stroked his cheek. "Do that for me tomorrow."*

"Remember, you can make as many mistakes as you need," Cameron said, pulling the makeup bib from

Owen's collar, "but if you keep me in these woods past sundown, I'll kill you."

Alex explained, "He had a bad experience in the woods."

"I had a bad experience," Cameron said, putting two fingers on Owen's lips to stop the inevitable question. "You can look it up later."

Alex turned to face them. "Are we ready?"

"Are we?" Cameron asked Owen,

Owen took in a deep breath and exhaled. "Yes."

"Remember, nothing is off limits." Alex took his seat and clipped on his mic. "I'll answer honestly."

Owen swallowed down his nervousness. "The same goes for you." He adjusted himself on the seat. "I want this to be a conversation." He looked at Cameron. "Jump in whenever you feel like it. Let's do this like we did yesterday. Call each other out on our bullshit."

"Okay," Cameron said, picking up a hand-held camera with a smile. "This isn't normal, but we can edit it out if we don't like it." He moved from camera to camera, turning them on. "Ready and action."

Owen looked directly into the camera Cameron had pointed at his face. "I'm Owen Sparks and I'm here, along with Cameron Matthews, to talk with Alex Sparks." He looked at Alex. "I'd thank you for doing this and being here, but this was your idea, including having me interview you. Why did you want to do this and why me?"

"Straight to the point." Alex laughed uncomfortably. "The truth is, I originally wanted to do this and have you do this because I wanted no secrets between me and you. I also wanted to give you the opportunity

to follow your dream that you didn't have because I abandoned you here."

Owen looked Alex in the eyes. "You said originally. What about now?"

"Now," Alex's face grew serious, "I don't want to be the horrible person my mother twisted me into anymore. I wronged a lot of people. I need to acknowledge and own the pain and hurt I caused, especially to those who called me a friend." Alex gave the camera a weak smile. "I can't expect them to accept my apology or let me back into their lives. I'm hoping they'll see this and know that I'm sorry."

Cameron jumped in, "Why is that important to you?"

"Because…" Alex paused, looking for the right words. "They deserve to know that the only reason I did any of it was because I wasn't a good person. I regret every hurtful act I did. I am truly sorry. It's not an excuse, but it was because I was so full of anger and resentment"

Owen probed further, "Who caused that anger and resentment?"

"My m—"

"Bullshit. Try again," Owen cut him off. He stared intensely at Alex. "The truth."

Alex shifted uncomfortably. "Fine. It was you and Uncle Terry," he spat out. "Uncle Terry brought you into my life and took you away! I fucking loved you! You were my world! Then you left me to go to school. I already knew I wasn't good enough for you. I only graduated high school by the skin of my teeth with your help. You didn't just leave me, you left me behind!"

Alex's body trembled with emotion. "Then I was on my own! Uncle Terry was gone. I was sleeping on benches and scrounging for food. I couldn't call you because my phone was dead, and I was too fucking angry to call you when I could afford to turn my phone back on. I was…" Alex paused, feeling his guilt. "I was too angry and embarrassed to try and contact you because I felt like a loser."

Alex's face reddened with anger and embarrassment. "Then I found out at Uncle Terry's funeral that you two were married! Do you know how foolish and stupid I felt?!" His hands formed into fists. His voice lowered. "Cameron helped dull that pain, but I refused to let myself be happy with him for the stupidest of reasons." Alex focused his eyes on Owen. "He wasn't you."

"Is that why you asked Dennis Childress to date you after you got engaged to Cameron Matthews?" Owen asked smoothly, trying not to show how affected he was by the outburst.

Alex looked at Cameron behind the camera he held. "I didn't do it to hurt Dennis or Cameron. I did it because I was selfish. I only saw what Dennis and Cameron could do for me. I did, and do, love them, but not the way they deserved to be loved."

"Is that why you confronted Billy Turner, which led to the now well-known break-up scene?" Owen pressed.

Alex opened his hands. "Sort of." He focused his eyes on Owen. "My mother had called me earlier that day demanding money that she allegedly needed. She

filled me with her poison and Billy and his boyfriend were there for me to unleash my anger on."

"If I hadn't found out," Cameron interjected, "would you have gone through with the wedding?"

Alex turned to Cameron's camera. "Honestly, I was surprised you said yes. The truth is, I would have done something else to screw up our relationship before the wedding if not after we were married. It's like we talked about, we really didn't love each other. We were only going through the motions."

"With as much pain as your Uncle Terry caused you, why did you come back here?" Owen asked.

Alex smiled warmly at Owen. "I hit rock bottom and as nice as Lexi Luscious was to let me stay at her place, I needed to get away from everyone and go someplace where I could heal. I needed to go someplace where I knew love. This was the last place I remembered truly feeling loved. This is the last place that I truly loved someone."

"Knowing what you know now, have you forgiven me? Have you let go of the anger and resentment toward me?" Owen asked.

"I still have some issues, but I'm working on them." Alex turned the question back on him. "Have you done the same for me?"

Owen hesitated before answering, "Yes."

# 26

# WHAT TO DO

ALEX HANDED CAMERON back his phone. "Thank you. I don't know if he'll forgive me, but at least he knows I'm sorry."

"I think it helped that you also apologized for picking that fight with Billy." Cameron set the phone aside and took Alex's hand. "Jordan will forgive you when Billy does." He saw the concern on Alex's face. "Billy will forgive you once he finds out you apologized to Jordan. It's a weird cycle."

Alex asked, "What about Carlos?"

"He's the one that needs forgiving," Cameron snapped. He saw the look Alex was giving him. "Okay, I need forgiveness from him, too. You, on the other hand, don't. You never did anything directly to Carlos."

Alex pleaded, "If this, being friends with me, is going to break you and Carlos up, I want you to choose him. He's good for you. He makes you happy."

"Oh, he makes me happy." Cameron grinned. "We're going to have one hell of a makeup session after this."

With a laugh, Alex shook his head. "You two have the strangest relationship."

"Unless you compare it to ours," Owen commented. Taking a seat next to Alex on the couch, he asked, "What did Cameron call me? Uncle boyfriend?"

Alex put an arm around Owen. "Yeah, I'm not calling you that."

"What did your property manager have to say?" Cameron asked, changing the subject.

Owen groaned. "Guess who the most hated people in the town are again? Rumors are spreading that we were in on it all with Danielle and Krystal." He settled in against Alex. "Xavier doesn't want us spending the night there and letting them know when we come and go for our safety."

"I was going to talk to you about us moving in here." Alex kissed the top of Owen's head. "Mr. and Mr. Sparks."

Cameron raised an eyebrow. "Wait so…" he trailed off when he saw Owen slightly shake his head. "You're moving here instead of back to California?"

"Who knows," Alex answered. "Depending on what happens with Owen's career and the court dates, I don't think we'll be settling down anywhere anytime soon."

Owen interlaced his fingers with Alex's. "I think it's safe to say we won't be staying in Springfield." He brought Alex's hand to his lips for a kiss. "That's a past we need to put behind us for a while."

"Agreed," Alex confirmed.

Cameron cleared his throat. "I have it on good authority that Jordan will be giving up his apartment soon if you want to move back, so you won't be too far from work."

"I told you I'm leaving the industry," Alex sighed. "Including content creation."

Cameron sat back with a smirk. "I wasn't talking to you."

"Why would I be working in California?" Owen asked, perplexed.

Cameron crossed his legs. "Owen Sparks, I have been authorized by my Aunt Lexi Luscious to offer you a position in the new media company she's launching."

"What?! That's amazing!" Owen exclaimed, nearly jumping from his seat. "Are you being serious right now?"

Cameron waved his hand flippantly about. "I'm being completely serious. Of course, Lexi wants you to work with Jordan and me, but she wants you." He fake yawned. "We'll send the contract to your manager, Alex, to look over."

"My manager, Alex?" Owen shot Alex a look.

Innocently, Alex proclaimed, "Don't look at me."

"You need someone you can trust looking out for you," Cameron explained. "Aunt Lexi isn't going to screw you, but there are plenty of people who will." He pointed at Alex. "At least when he screws you, it ends in an orgasm."

Owen let the words sink in. "It makes sense, I guess."

"I'll help until you learn to do it yourself or find a real manager," Alex amended. "I need to find my way, maybe go to school or something."

Conspiratorially, Cameron said, "You mean like video editing and producing for Aunt Lexi's company?" He failed to look innocently at Alex's shocked expression. "What? You're a great video editor, and you've done great work here making sure the lighting and sound are perfect."

Alex shook his head. "But—"

Sharply, Cameron cut Alex off. "If you're going to give me a but, I'd better be able to kiss it, lick it, or fuck it." Calmer, he said, "Just think about it. You already said your property management company runs itself and Owen is going to be traveling for work, so why not be by his side helping him?"

"It makes sense," Owen took Alex's hand. "At least for a little while."

Cameron repeated, "Just think about it."

"Fine," Alex grumbled. "I'll think about it." He brought Owen's hands to his lips for a kiss.

"Good, now we need to talk about Mark's and Hunter's wedding." Cameron let out an annoying sigh of frustration.

Alex shook his head. "I'm not going."

"We're going." Owen countered. "You'll regret it if we don't." He looked Alex in the eyes. "The grooms want you there. To hell with everyone else. Don't hurt your friends by not showing up to their wedding because you're too scared to face everyone else."

Alex pulled Owen close. "As long as you are by my side."

"Speaking of which," Cameron interjected, "I'm going to need both of you to help me during the wedding." Alex and Owen turned their attention to him. "Jordan is not to be left alone with Billy, no matter what, until after the wedding. He's going to need a lot of support from us and I'm trusting you two can help me."

Alex nodded. "If he wants it, I'll give it to him. I won't force my presence on him."

"I'll do what I can." Owen then asked curiously, "What's going on?"

Cameron debated a moment before saying, "Jordan is working on a top-secret project as a present for Billy. I'm surprised he kept it a secret from Billy this long. As far as I know, only Aunt Lexi and I know the full details of it." Cameron's voice went soft. "You two are the only people that'll understand what they'll be going through." He turned his focus on Owen. "Especially you."

"No good deed," Owen whispered, understanding Cameron's meaning.

# FINAL THOUGHTS

*T*HIS IS SURREAL, Owen thought, sitting on the stool across from Alex as Cameron adjusted the lighting. *After we finish this interview, we're going to start packing up everything and by tomorrow afternoon, this place will no longer be my home and my prison.*

Turning the cameras on, Cameron said, "Okay, we're ready." He came around and took his seat between Owen and Alex. Adjusting his clothes, he said, "Ready when you are."

"I'm ready," Alex said, with a hint of nervousness.

Owen closed his eyes, mentally counted to ten, opened his eyes, then said, "I'm Owen Sparks and I'm back here with Cameron Matthews and Alex Sparks for our post-interview discussion." He turned his attention to Alex. "You've shared with us your story, told us every awful thing you've done, stated that you don't want forgiveness, that you want the world to know that you are sorry and that if people forgive you that would be great, but you don't expect anyone to. Is there anything else you'd like to add?"

"Yes." Alex stiffened up. "I've done a lot of soul searching and come to the decision that it's time for me to leave the adult film industry. I need to forge a new path that brings me happiness. I don't know exactly what that is yet, but I'm hoping that you'll be by my side as I make that journey."

Cameron turned his focus to Owen. "What do you say, Owen? After hearing everything Alex has been through and every awful thing he has done, will you stay by his side?"

Owen looked directly at Alex. "I'm no angel, and it would be foolish to expect Alex to be one. I know who Alex was when we were younger. I now know who he was when we were apart. I know who he is now and I look forward to getting to know who he becomes." He smiled at Alex. "So to answer that question is yes. I will stay by Alex's side on his journey if he'll stay beside me on mine."

"Of course I will." Alex returned the smile, then turned to Cameron. "What about you? Do you still want to be associated with me after hearing everything?"

Cameron took a moment to gather his words. "I shouldn't, but I do. Despite everything, I still remember you in that hospital room. That's when I saw who you really were and I realized I never truly knew you. I only knew a distorted version of you that you shared when we were together because you felt that's what you had to do. Like Owen, I'm looking forward to getting to know who you become."

Cameron reached over and put a hand on Owen's knee. "I also look forward to getting to know you better. I have enjoyed getting to know you during this project. In the short time we've been together, I have come to call you a friend and consider you family. I hope you feel the same."

"I do." Owen put his hand on Cameron's. "And I truly thank you for everything you and your Aunt Lexi have done for Alex and me."

Alex added, "That goes for me as well. Who knows where I would be if you two hadn't stepped up to help me when you did."

"I did some research and there is one more question I have to ask." Cameron gave Owen's knee a squeeze before taking back his hand. He pointed at Owen. "You're Owen Sparks." He pointed at Alex. "You're Alex Sparks. Your Uncle Terry who married," he pointed at Owen, "you, had a last name of Jones. You changed your name when you got married. Why is your last name Sparks instead of Jones?"

Realization hit Alex. "Yeah, why isn't your last name Jones?"

"You caught that." Owen shifted uncomfortably. "After I married Terry Jones, there was a ton of red tape we were facing in order to change my name. I commented on how I dreaded ever having to do it again. Really, we didn't have to change my name, but Terry was old-fashioned. That's what married couples did when he was growing up, and I didn't know any better."

Owen let out a soft laugh. "Terry's attorney took care of all the paperwork for us. When everything

was processed, I assumed my new last name was going to be Jones, but it was Sparks. When I asked Terry about it, he said he didn't think I should have to change my name again, either."

Owen looked fondly at Alex. "He said he knew we'd end up together eventually, so why not get a head start on the paperwork?"

"Are you two getting married?" Cameron asked, shocked.

Alex answered, "Yes."

"Eventually," Owen added. "We're not there yet, but we will be."

Cameron nodded. "I get that."

"And that concludes this interview." Owen looked at the camera with a smile. "We thank you for watching."

# MOVING ON

**O**WEN STROLLED THROUGH the house that was once his salvation, his home, and ultimately his prison. The small box truck was laden with boxes of memories. Monday, professional movers would come and pack up the furniture and cart it away to storage.

"It's surreal," Alex said, hugging Owen from behind. "This is the place we first met. Where we fell in love. Shared our first kiss. Where we first discovered the joys of gay sex."

Owen lightly jabbed Alex in the ribs. "Pervert." He leaned back against Alex. "It's where we found each other again and we started healing."

"I don't want to leave, but I can't stay here any longer." Owen pulled Alex's hands tighter around him. "Maybe one day we'll be able to come back here and it won't hurt so much."

Alex rested his chin on Owen's shoulder. "Terry never meant for us to stay here. He wanted us to get out of this hellhole of a town. He wanted this place to be somewhere we could feel safe, some place for us to come back to if we needed to."

"Maybe this place could be that for others," Owen said wistfully. "Maybe we could turn this place into a community center of sorts. This town is changing, whether they like it or not. There are going to be kids out there like me and you that will need safe places and people like Terry and my dad that need help."

Alex murmured in his ear, "I like that idea. Uncle Terry would like that idea."

"Excuse me." Cameron stepped into the room. "I hate to interrupt this touching moment, but we need to go. It's getting dark, and we're in the woods. In a town that doesn't like you two very much at the moment."

Alex kissed Owen on the cheek. "Come on. Let's go start our lives together."

# LEXI'S HOTEL ROOM

**A**LEX STOOD NERVOUSLY in Lexi's hotel room, waiting for her to scold him. Owen stood beside him, holding his hand. She said nothing as she sipped her wine and studied him with her caring, yet angry, eyes. It wasn't lost on Alex that he finally knew what it felt like to be a child under the gaze of an upset mother.

"Not to interrupt this obviously needed uncomfortable situation for Alex," Owen spoke up, "but I'd like to get to what you wanted to talk to me about."

Lexi's lips curled into a satisfied smile. She casually set her wine glass aside. "I like you. You've got balls. Big ones."

"I can vouch that he has balls," Alex spoke up, trying to add some levity to the situation. Owen covered his face with his free hand. Lexi gave him a scathing glare. Cameron chuckled. "I'll be quiet now."

Lexi focused on Alex. "Let's get it over with." She waved her hand about in an airy gesture. She said the words, but they had no bite to them. "What were you thinking? How could you disappear? After all I've done for you, you couldn't pick up a phone and call to tell me you're alright? Yadda. Yadda. Yadda."

"You're not mad?" Alex asked, shocked.

Lexi picked her glass up and finished the rest of her wine. "I am, but I also know you did what you did because you had to. Add in your mother and sister trying to kill you for insurance money, them being arrested for fraud, and finding out everything your Uncle Owen was dealing with, I'll forgo mad for now."

"I'm only his uncle by marriage," Owen interjected. "Not blood. Really, I'm only his uncle on paper."

Lexi teased, "And I bet he's your daddy in bed."

"Wow," Owen blushed. "Was not expecting that one."

Lexi motioned them to sit. "I've been sitting on that one since Cameron told me about your little situation." She cleared her throat. "Let's get right to the point. I've seen the raw footage and I love it. What I love most about it is the interactions between the three of you." She pointed to Owen, Alex, and then Cameron. "You make a great team. You were no-nonsense, calling each other out on bullshit, and completely raw. I want you three to do a roundtable chat about the issues our community is facing."

Lexi paused to let her idea settle in. "I want you to bring in special guests to join you and I also want you to do your own series of interviews with Alex by your side." She watched Alex's eyes grow big, then added, "As your producer."

"I'll do it," Owen said without hesitation. "Under one condition."

With a curious look, Lexi said, "Go on."

"I need a mentor, actually I need a lot of mentors," Owen admitted. "If it weren't for Cameron tricking me, none of what we did would have happened."

Lexi waved an imaginary wand around. "Done. You'll have Cameron, me, and Jordan."

"Hey," Cameron spoke up. "Don't I get a say in all this? What if Jordan says no? I know we agreed to work with him but mentor?"

"What is this? Your first day knowing me?" Lexi cocked her head at Cameron in disbelief. "After the stunts you two pulled for these stories, you're lucky I haven't skinned you both alive."

"Point of order." Alex raised his hand. "I didn't say yes."

Owen patted Alex's knee. "You did when I said yes."

"Owen, I can tell you and I are going to get along fabulously." Lexi chuckled. "Why don't you two head to your room and get some rest? Tomorrow is going to be a big day."

Owen stood, pulling Alex along with him. "Thank you again for everything you've done for Alex and me. It really means a lot to us."

"You two are family. I'll do anything for my family." Lexi stood and hugged them both. "Keep him on his toes," she said to Owen. "Keep making his toes curl," she said to Alex. To Cameron, she said, "Jordan is arriving early in the morning and he isn't disturbing my beauty sleep." She gave Cameron a pointed look. "Do we understand each other?"

Cameron pulled out his phone. "I'll text him to come to my room instead of yours."

# OWEN TAKES RESPONSIBILITY

**T**HE MOMENT THE hotel room door closed, Alex slid an arm around Owen's waist and pulled him close. "Do you like volunteering me for things?" he growled playfully in Owen's ear. He cupped Owen's crotch with his other hand. "Does it make you hard?" He ground his hard cock into Owen's ass. "It makes me hard."

"Alex…" Owen's words turned to a moan with the soft graze of Alex's teeth on his neck.

Alex nipped Owen's ear. "We're in our own hotel room. You don't have to worry about Cameron or anyone else hearing you."

"I should take responsibility for causing this." Owen ground his ass back into Alex.

Alex's hands alleviated Owen of his shirt. "How should I punish you for causing me such an obscene problem?"

"Pleasurably," Owen answered seductively, kicking his shoes off as he spun around.

Slipping two fingers into the top of Owen's pants, Alex pulled him flush. With his other hand, he gripped the back of Owen's head. "When I'm done, you'll be lucky if you can walk tomorrow." He kissed Owen vehemently, his tongue a welcomed invasion into Owen's mouth. Pulling back, he grazed his teeth over Owen's bottom lip. "You're wearing too many clothes." He popped the top button of Owen's jeans. "You're going to be a good boy and take your punishment, aren't you?"

"Of course," Owen groaned as he pushed down his pants and underwear.

With his hands under Owen's arms, Alex lifted him up, then unceremoniously tossed him on the bed. "You're taking too long." Owen's socks, pants, and underwear went flying behind Alex. "Delaying your punishment." Alex pulled his shirt off and tossed it aside. "There will be consequences for that."

"What sort of consequences?" Owen asked lustfully, scooting to the center of the bed.

Taking in Owen's naked body, Alex kicked his shoes off while unbuttoning his jeans. "I haven't decided yet." His jeans and underwear fell to the floor. "I'm sure we'll both enjoy it." Stepping out of his clothes, he crawled on top of Owen. He flicked his tongue over Owen's lips. "What am I going to do with you?"

"Anything you want." Owen pulled him down into a hungry kiss.

Hungrily they kissed with Alex grinding his hard cock into Owen. Owen held him tight, running his hands along the hard, defined lines of Alex's back.

Their tongues and bodies tangled. Owen pressed his hard, dripping cock up into Alex.

"Naughty," Alex admonished, taking Owen's hands and pinning them above his head. Alex growled, "Keep them there, or I'll find something to tie them up with."

Owen trembled with desire. "Yes, sir."

Alex started with a light kiss on the lips. Brushing his stubbled cheek along Owen's skin, he whispered in Owen's ear, "Don't hold back. I want everyone in this hotel to hear how good I'm making you feel." He flicked his tongue over Owen's ear. "If you want me to stop, just say coconut. Understand?"

"Yes, sir." Owen then let out a gasp at the gentle bite on his neck. "No marks! Wedding tomorrow!"

Alex flicked his tongue over the spot he bit. "No marks," Alex slipped down Owen's body to his nipple, "that can be seen, you mean." Owen gasped at the graze of Alex's teeth over his nub. "I love how sensitive you are."

"Alex!" Owen exclaimed at the pleasurable pain of Alex's teeth on his left nipple while Alex's right hand slowly traced the outline of his right nipple. "You're evil." Instantly, Owen felt joyous regret at his words.

Alex's tongue swirled and flicked across the tiny nub. His right hand slowly traced Owen's quivering body. When Owen's breathing became too rigid and rough, Alex stopped and slowly kissed his way across Owen's chest. He waited until Owen's breath calmed, then latched on Owen's right nipple, flooding his body with pleasure once again.

"You son of a bitch—fuck!" Owen cursed, catching himself from moving his arms as his body twisted in pleasure.

Alex smiled, flicking his tongue over the sensitive spot. He began moving his way down, ravaging Owen's body with rapid flicks of his tongue along with gentle bites. He would only pause and turn to kisses when Owen's breathing got too ragged or his body grew too wild to control.

"Alex, please," Owen moaned desperately, catching his breath, "have mercy."

Between kisses along Owen's stomach, Alex asked, "I wonder how many times I can bring you to the brink."

"Alex, don't you dare!" Owen exclaimed, watching Alex move down between his legs. "We need our rest for tomorrow!"

Alex licked from the base of Owen's cock to the tip. "You've got the safe word."

Alex took the crown of Owen's cock in his mouth and swirled his tongue over it. He deliberately took Owen's cock slowly into his mouth, letting his tongue explore and taste the rock-hard flesh. Owen moaned in ecstasy above him and finally let out a groan of satisfaction when Alex had swallowed him whole.

Alex's hands roamed up Owen's body. His left fingers found Owen's left nipple to slowly tease it with a whisper of touches. Two of his right fingers slipped into Owen's moaning mouth, which he eagerly sucked and licked in contrast to Alex's deliberate slow glide along his cock.

Alex allowed Owen to suckle on his fingers while he continued slowly nurse Owen's cock until felt the slight throb of his dick and slight twitch that Alex knew all too well indicated how close Owen was to climaxing. Owen groaned around Alex's fingers in dismay at Alex robbing him of his release by pulling off his cock.

"Not yet, my pretty," Alex announced in a villainous tone. "I'm not done with you."

Moving up to lay beside Owen's body, he pulled his fingers from Owen's mouth, only to cover it with his own to fiercely kiss him. Alex's spit-slick fingers traveled down Owen's body to slip between his legs and under him, to push between his cheeks and stroke along his crevice.

Owen desperately cried out into the kiss as first one finger, then the next, slipped into him. He spread his legs as wide as he could and arched his hips up to allow Alex easier access. He gasped when Alex's fingers began caressing that special spot inside of him.

"How does it feel?" Alex asked devilishly, trying to hold on to Owen's writhing body. "Good?"

Owen struggled to form words, eventually letting out a broken, "A-Alex … too … ugh!" Owen's body jolted. "Much,"

"Then say the word to have me stop," Alex growled in Owen's ear. "Go ahead, say it and I'll stop your punishment and let you release."

Between shudders, Owen snapped, "Shut up … ugh! And f-f-fuck … fuck! Me!"

"All in due time." Alex nuzzled Owen's cheek. "I think you've had enough of this." He pulled his fingers

from Owen's tight, warm insides. Owen whimpered at the emptiness. Alex kissed him lightly on the lips. "Flip over onto your stomach."

Rolling over, Owen grumbled, "Fucking bossy tops." That earned him a playful smack on his ass. "Hey!"

"Oh, did that hurt?" Alex ran a hand over Owen's ass. "Let me kiss it and make it better." He moved back down between Owen's legs. He rained down kisses over Owen's lightly furry bottom. Then, without warning, he gently bit Owen's left cheek.

"Ouch!" Owen thrust his hips backward to turn, but Alex took advantage of the raised butt to spread Owen's cheeks to mercilessly start swirling and swiping his tongue along his crevice. "Oh, fuck." Owen purred, arching his hips up. "Yeah, that. That right there."

Alex pressed his tongue into Owen, feeling how relaxed yet tight he was. He ran a soothing hand up along Owen's back. He needed to be in Owen, but what he needed more was to hear Owen moan his name.

"Don't move or else," Alex vaguely threatened, lightly smacking Owen's ass. He got off the bed and went to the welcome basket Lexi arranged to have in their room. Finding the small bottle of lube, he quickly broke the safety seals, then returned to kneel between Owen's legs.

Alex ran his free hand over Owen's cheeks. "Such a lovely sight." He spread Owen's cheeks and driz-zled lube along his crack, then pushed his own hard dick under the stream. Replacing the top, he tossed

the lube aside and covered Owen's body, nestling his cock between his slicked-up cheeks.

Reaching along Owen's arms, Alex interlaced their fingers. He moved his hips, sliding his cock along Owen's crack. "Tell me, Owen," he growled huskily in Owen's ear, "do you want my cock in your ass?"

"Yes," Owen gasped, pushing his ass back to try to catch Alex's dick.

Alex swirled his tongue over the back of Owen's neck. "I can't hear you."

"Yes!" Owen shouted, thrusting his ass back again.

Alex gently chewed on Owen's ear. "Yes, what?" he asked teasingly.

"Ugh!" Owen tried to spear himself on Alex's cock, but failed. "Yes! I want your cock in my ass!"

Alex chuckled, licking a line down Owen's neck. "Whose cock do you want in your ass?"

"Sexy jerk," Owen huffed through clenched teeth. He took in a deep breath, then shouted at the top of his lungs, "I want your dick in my ass, Alex!"

Playfully, Alex asked, "Alex who?"

"I swear if you don't put your fucking cock in me right now, you'll regret it!" Owen threatened.

A few well-aimed thrusts and the head of Alex's cock slipped into Owen. "Is this what you wanted, baby?" Owen grunted, pushing back, sinking more of Alex into him. "I'll take that as a yes." Alex pushed deeper into Owen's tight confines until he was fully in. "Mm, you're so tight and warm. I could stay like this all night."

"If you don't fuck me," Owen warned. "Oh, Fuck!" he cried out when Alex sucked on the back of his neck. "No marks!"

Alex slowly raised his hips, then lowered them down. "No one's going to be looking at the back of your neck." He slowly raised his hips back up and down. "Fine, but I'm going to take my time." He raised his hips, so only the head of his cock stayed in Owen. "Maybe take all night."

"I'm going to clench and rip your dick off if you don't—holy fuck!" Owen shouted when Alex slammed back into him. "Bastard," he huffed.

Alex kissed Owen's cheek. "Why don't you lay there and enjoy your punishment like a good boy?" He slowly humped Owen.

"Alex, please. I need it," Owen pleaded. "Fuck me."

Alex steadily pumped into Owen. He kissed Owen's shoulder. "Only because I can't stand to see you suffer." He kissed along Owen's back. "I'll save the rest of your punishment for another night." Alex tightened his grip on Owen's hands. "Next time, there will be rope and toys."

"Next time," Owen gasped, "I'm doing this to you!"

Alex began picking up speed. He could feel Owen's body pushing and pulling him in and out. "Yeah? Doesn't sound like punishment to me." Alex slammed hard into Owen. "You teasing my body? Sounds like heaven to me." He resumed his steady pumping. "I'm ready when you are." He leaned down and whispered into Owen's ear, "Don't forget to use toys."

"Oh, I'm going to go shopping specifically for toys to use on you," Owen grunted, meeting Alex's thrusts.

"That spot, right there." Owen rolled his shoulders. "Yeah, fuck!"

Alex pounded harder and faster. "That spot?" He rolled his hips while thrusting. "Or that spot?"

"Both," Owen grunted. "Fuck, I feel like I'm about to cum." Alex leaned down and latched onto Owen's shoulder with his teeth. "Bastard!"

Releasing Owen's shoulder, Alex ordered, "Not until I'm done making you moan."

"Come on, Alex." Owen pushed back harder against Alex. "You know you want to blow your load in me. You know you want to feel your cock pulsing in me while I shoot my load."

Alex began thrusting harder and faster. "I can feel you squeezing my cock with your ass, you sneaky little bitch," he leaned down and growled in Owen's ear. "You're trying to make me cum." Alex nuzzled Owen's cheek. "If you want me to cum, all you have to do is ask." He kissed Owen's cheek. "Properly."

"Alex, please," Owen panted.

Alex punctuated his words with a hard thrust. "I said properly and loud enough for me to hear." He thrust hard into Owen again. "I'm a little hard of hearing."

"Alex, please, fucking cum in me!" Owen shouted. "Alex, I want you to shoot your load in me!"

Alex leaned down and kissed Owen's cheek. "Good boy." He began jackhammering into Owen. "So you know, we're not done once I cum."

"Fuck! Yes! Pound me!" Owen tossed his head back.

Alex felt his orgasm building. "Yeah, baby." He captured Owen's mouth and kissed him hungrily. His

body tensed. "Owen," he whimpered into the kiss. He brought their hands together under Owen and held him tight. His orgasm pulsed, blasting his load deep into Owen. "Owen," he whimpered again, pulling Owen tighter.

"Fuck, I needed that." Alex relaxed his grip on Owen. He kissed Owen. "Now for you." He rolled them over so Owen lay on top of him. "Stay," he ordered, putting an arm around Owen's waist and sitting up. He stacked the pillows behind him. "Let's see how far you shoot with my dick still in you."

Owen moaned at the feel of Alex's hand on his cock. "Don't drag it out," he pleaded, running his hand along Alex's arms. He shuddered at Alex's slow stroke of his cock.

"You're pouring out precum like a faucet." Alex ran his hand over the crown to gather Owen's juices to spread across his dick. "How badly do you want to cum, baby?"

Owen leaned his head back to try to kiss Alex. "Alex, don't be cruel."

"Fine. It is your orgasm, after all." Alex kissed Owen.

Alex's hand pumped Owen's cock, gliding over the crown occasionally to gather more precum. Owen moaned into the kiss. He reached back and pulled Alex harder into the kiss. He moved his hips to fuck Alex's stroking hand. Suddenly he cried out in the kiss and thrust his hips up as his stomach and chest were coated in his sticky warm climax.

Owen jolted a few more times before falling back onto Alex's chest. He released Alex's mouth from the

kiss and tried to catch his breath. "Bastard," he flung out between breaths. "Asshole."

"You know you enjoyed every minute of it." Alex ran his hand over Owen's stomach, smearing in his load. "You would have said banana if you wanted me to stop."

Owen tried to get up, but Alex held him down. "The word was coconut!"

"I know." Alex kissed Owen's temple. "Let's stay like this for a bit then get cleaned up."

Owen groaned. "Your dick is still inside me."

"Better get used to it." Alex patted Owen's soft belly. "I think it likes it in there."

# 31

# COFFEE TALK

OWEN NEEDED COFFEE. Real coffee, not the weak stuff they provided in the hotel room. Riding the elevator down, he prayed that they served halfway decent coffee downstairs at the breakfast the hotel provided. He needed it after waking up and finding he was in a text thread with the topic of discussion being what he and Alex did the night before.

He groaned in embarrassment going through the text thread.

[Cameron: Did you hear all that noise on the floor last night?]

[Lexi: I did. It sounded like something I wanted to get on camera. Sounded HOT!]

[Jordan: It's too early to be talking about this stuff. Cameron, hurry up in the bathroom. I'm going down to breakfast.]

[Cameron: It takes time for me come out presentable. Go grab a table for five, but I think only four of us are eating. I'm pretty sure someone is still stuffed from last night.]

[Lexi: Did you know the hotel called my room because the people below them were complaining about the noise?]

[Cameron: I almost barged in to watch.]

[Jordan: Seriously too early. Cameron, you look pretty enough for breakfast. Lexi, really? I got us a table. Hurry up.]

[Lexi: Hush, Jordan. Cameron, were they this loud when you were staying with them?]

[Cameron: I don't think they had sex while I was there. Now I know why. Owen, you may want to soundproof your condo.]

[Jordan: Who is Owen?]

[Cameron: The one that made all those noises last night! Oh, wait, you missed that. Whoops! You'll see him at breakfast.]

[Lexi: He'll be easy to spot. He'll be the one walking funny… if he can walk.]

[Alex: He can walk and he saw the text. He punched me and is looking for coffee. Cameron, you better hope he's in a better mood once he's caffeinated.]

[Jordan: I have a table for five. Get your asses down here.]

Owen tucked his phone into his pocket when the elevator doors opened and went straight to the restaurant. *I'll make them pay. I'll make them all pay.* Owen ran a hand through his hair. *Fuck. Why do I always sound like some cartoon supervillain before my coffee?* He smiled at the host and tried to keep the gruffness out of his voice. "I'm joining a table for five. Um, I think it's under Jordan… fuck, what is his last name?"

"I just sat that table." The host beamed at him. "Follow me."

He followed the perky host to the lone person sitting at a huge round table. *Fuck.* Owen mentally cursed. *I forgot I'd be the only one with Jordan.*

"Here you go, sir." The host pulled a chair out for Owen.

"Thank you." Owen looked uncertainly at Jordan. *Fuck. He doesn't know who I am.* He thrust out his hand to Jordan. "Owen Sparks."

Jordan looked at the hand, then at Owen. Owen's stomach knotted. Jordan stood and took his hand. "Jordan Hudson. Pleasure to meet you." He smiled warmly at Owen. "I ordered you a coffee when I got seated." Jordan sat down. "I heard you had quite a night. In fact, I hear half the hotel heard you had quite a night."

"You must help me plot my revenge," Owen said, taking his seat. Grimacing, he added, "Sorry, I haven't been caffeinated yet so I sound like a cartoon supervillain."

Jordan laughed, "Or a mildly inconvenienced gay man."

"I heard you're in desperate need of good coffee," their server said, filling the cup in front of Owen.

Owen groaned, "Don't tell me you know, too."

"Know what?" The server asked, filling Jordan's cup.

Jordan smiled. "Thank you, and you don't want to know."

"This is going to be my fun table this morning, isn't it?" the server asked, walking away before they could answer.

Owen prepared his coffee and took a long, healthy sip. "Okay, I think I can function now."

"Good." Jordan took a sip of his coffee. "I'm glad it's just the two of us. I wanted to get your advice on something."

Puzzled, Owen asked, "My advice?"

"Cameron gave me the short version of what went on with you and Alex." Jordan began turning his cup on the table. "In order to help Alex, you had to hurt him and you lost Alex for a time because of it." He looked at Owen with pleading eyes. "How did you go on without Alex? With him hating you?"

Owen reached out and touched Jordan's arm. "What's going on?"

"You know my boyfriend is Billy." Jordan smiled brightly when he said, "Billy Turner. He means everything to me, and I did the one thing I promised him

I'd do." He wiped away a tear. "The problem is in order for me to do what I promised him, I had to make and keep a promise to someone else that will destroy Billy." With a slight tremble in his voice, Jordan admitted, "I'm scared he'll leave me."

Owen patted Jordan's arm. "I see." He thought for a moment. "I really don't know you or Billy, but you told me something already." Owen offered him a smile. "You love Billy. What I need to know is, does Billy love you?"

"Without a question." Jordan smiled brightly. "He calls me his teddy bear."

Owen nodded, letting go of Jordan's arm. "That's cute. What do you call him?"

"I really didn't have a nickname for him," Jordan answered, a hint of shame in his voice. "I usually called him something generic, like baby or pookie."

Smiling, Owen pressed, "But you do now?"

"Yeah." Jordan's face brightened. "I can't wait for him to hear it."

Studying Jordan, Owen finished his coffee, then motioned the server over. "It sounds like Billy is very special to you." He smiled at the server as they filled his cup, then Jordan's. "Thank you." Fixing his coffee, Owen asked, "Could you tell me more about Billy? What's the single thing you love about Billy?"

"It's that he's Billy." Jordan's face lit up. "You'll understand once you meet him. He has this innocence about him that draws you in. Billy is like that first ray of sunlight piercing through a storm, like a warm fluffy blanket on a cold night."

Stirring his coffee, Owen asked, "Why is he with you?"

"What?!" Jordan nearly knocked over his coffee. "Because I love him and he loves me."

"Okay, one more thing." Owen took a long, healthy sip of his coffee. "Just an observation." He sat his cup down. "You're not really afraid Billy will leave you. You're worried about when he'll forgive you and whether he'll say yes."

Jordan's protest died on his lips. He smiled. "You got me to open up without even trying. You're good."

"So I'm told." Owen smiled back. "I'm looking forward to learning more from you." He took Jordan's hand. "For what it's worth, I think he'll say yes."

Jordan squeezed Owen's hand. "He has to forgive me first."

"He will," Owen reassured him.

"Thanks." Jordan sighed. "For what it's worth, I think he'll forgive Alex, too. I pretty much have."

Owen stared down into his coffee. "I appreciate that."

"Good morning." Cameron walked up and put a hand on Owen's and Jordan's shoulders. "What are we talking about, boys?" He took a seat beside Jordan.

Jordan sipped his coffee casually. "Just plotting your demise."

"What did I do?" Cameron feigned innocence.

Owen scowled at Cameron. "You know what you did."

"And I heard what you did," Cameron laughed. "Bravo."

Jordan looked at Owen. "I heard you were, um, loud."

Owen buried his head in his hands. "Don't remind me."

# BRUTAL HONESTY

**H**OLDING THE ELEVATOR door open for Lexi, Alex suggestively asked, "Going down?"

"Not on you," she cheekily responded as she got on.

Laughing, Alex released the door. "Fair"

"You two put on quite a performance last night." Lexi smirked. "Good thing I put your room between mine and Cameron's."

Hitting the ground button, Alex let out a bark of laughter. "The sounds that are going to be coming from this floor tonight."

"You mean from all the fighting and crying?" Lexi sighed. "How is your relationship with your uncle the normal one in this group?"

Alex quickly clarified, "He's only my uncle by marriage."

"Noted," Lexi said with a sly grin.

Silence lingered between them before Alex finally spoke. "Lexi, I have to ask, because you barely tolerated me while I was dating Cameron." Looking at

Lexi through her reflection in the stainless steel doors. "Why did you help me? Why are you still helping me? Owen, I get, but why me?"

"Let's sit in the lobby for a minute." Lexi motioned to the opening elevator doors. "I prefer to be comfortable when I'm brutally honest."

Alex led the way to a corner spot with plush chairs and lush greenery shielding them from view. "I assume this is okay?"

"Perfect." Lexi took a seat and waited for Alex to get comfortable before she began. "I'm not going to sugarcoat this, so let me know when you're ready."

Alex took in a deep breath, held it, then let it out. "Ready."

"No, Alex, I did not like you when you were with Cameron. To be honest, I barely liked Cameron then," Lexi said unapologetically. "You were a horrible person and an even worse boyfriend to my nephew. I smiled politely and kept my mouth shut when Cameron announced your engagement, because I knew he'd see the truth of who you were or you'd do something to fuck it up." She took a moment to take a breath. "You did both. Thank you for that."

Alex flinched. "Ouch."

"In the hospital, I saw a new side to you," Lexi continued. "Your hard exterior was cracked open, and we got to see your soft center." Her eyes were a blend of sympathy and sadness. "I saw the scared little boy reaching out for his mama so she could kiss his boo-boo and she was nowhere to be found. I saw the broken man that had no one left to reach out to

but his ex-fiancé." Lexi leaned forward and put a hand on his knee. "I finally understood."

Alex covered her hand with his, but said nothing. "You wanted to be happy and loved, but didn't know how to let yourself. You were the way you were because you were so full of anger and bitterness, that's all that came out of you. I saw someone hurting who needed help, that didn't have anyone to ask, and didn't know how to ask."

She gave Alex's knee a squeeze. "I saw someone who needed me and someone I needed to help. Whether they wanted it or not." She patted his knee, then sat up straight. "Like someone did for me way back when."

Alex smiled slightly. "Would you approve of this Alex marrying Cameron?"

"Absolutely not." Lexi laughed at his hurt expression. "Now that I've met Owen and seen," she winked, "and heard you two together, it's obvious to see you two belong together."

Alex smiled to himself. "My rooster crows for him and his bull moos for me."

"What does that mean?" Lexi held up a hand to stop him from answering. "No. No. I'd rather not know."

Alex laughed. "We should get to breakfast." He pointed to Cameron crossing the lobby. "There goes Cameron. One of us needs to protect him from Owen."

"That boy needs to grab himself by the shoulders and yank his head out his ass." Lexi huffed. She shrugged at Alex's amused expression. "Billy's influence." She dismissed it with a wave. "He needs to make

up with Carlos already. Why do they insist on pissing each other off?"

Alex snorted. "Make-up sex." He grew serious when he saw Lexi was not amused. "I'll do what I can to help fix them." A second later, he added, "And help Jordan and Billy however I can. I don't know what's going on, but it seems like everyone is preparing for the worst."

"The worst, then the best." Lexi debated whether to divulge the secret. "Remember the Country Boyz murders?" Alex nodded. "Besides Billy, the only other survivor is a guy named Shadow that we couldn't find."

Alex thought for a second. "Don't you mean suspected survivor? No one has conf…" Alex's eyes went wide. "Jordan found him!?"

"Keep your voice down," Lexi admonished. She checked to see if they had drawn anyone's attention. "The truth is, Shadow found Jordan, and Jordan interviewed him with the agreement that he not tell Billy where he is."

Alex leaned back. "Fuck."

"I thought, maybe, since your situation was sort of like Billy's, that maybe you could…" She let the unfinished question hang in the air.

Alex nodded. "If he'll listen."

"He'll listen because you're going to start off with what I'm going to tell you." Lexi smiled conspiratorially.

# 33

# SECRET DEAL

**O**WEN CASUALLY WATCHED Carlos from afar. *I just need five minutes alone with him.* The reception was slowly coming to an end. Mark and Hunter were on the dance floor looking fondly into each other's eyes as they held each other. *One day, that'll be me and Alex.* He sipped his drink. *Maybe in a year or two.* He casually handed his drink over to Alex when he saw Carlos head into the house alone. "I've got to pee."

He made his way through the thinning crowd. He caught sight of Carlos heading down a hallway and followed. Carlos ducked into a room. Gathering his strength, he knocked on the door. When no response came, he opened the door and stepped inside. Closing the door behind him, he gathered his courage.

*I can do this.* He told himself. *For Cameron.*

He jumped at the sound of a toilet flushing. He heard the faucet going, then a few moments later, the door to the en-suite bathroom opened. Carlos's expression went from surprise to confusion, and then finally settled on anger as he realized who he was in the room with.

"What are you doing in my room?" Carlos demanded. He pointed to the door behind Owen. "Get out."

Owen swallowed hard. "I wanted to talk to you."

"I don't want to talk to you or Alex." Carlos went to push past Owen.

Owen grabbed him by the arm. "Please, don't," he looked at his hand holding Carlos's muscular toned arm, then at Carlos's scowling face. "Hit me."

"I'm not going to hit you." Carlos yanked his arm away. "Isn't it enough that your date is trying to steal my boyfriend and had the nerve to show up to the wedding with you? Which reminds me, who are you? One of his little minions?"

Owen refused to be intimidated or insulted. He knew Carlos was angry and just lashing out. "I'm Owen. Alex's date and boyfriend," he answered calmly. "Alex is here because I made him and because the grooms want him here." Not liking Owen's answers, Carlos reached for the door. "Alex isn't trying to steal Cameron from you." Carlos's hand rested on the doorknob. "He couldn't if he wanted. Cameron is only interested in you."

"Why should I believe you?" Carlos asked, hand still on the doorknob.

Owen decided brutal honesty was best. "Because I would cut Alex's balls off if he even thought about leaving me again." Carlos looked at him. "Then I would cut off Cameron's."

"You're serious." Carlos let go of the door. "So you're dating Alex. How did you meet him?"

Owen gave a weak smile. "Our history and relationship are complicated." Puzzled, he looked at Carlos. "Did Cameron not tell you anything?"

"No." Carlos bit the inside of his cheek. "He didn't tell me anything. I know I shouldn't worry or get jealous." He sighed. "He's the first person I really cared about. I moved out here to be with him. I can see us being happy together for a very long time, but he likes to push my buttons. Normally it's small things, and I don't mind because of the makeup sex, but this has been going on…"

Owen put a comforting hand on his shoulder. "But this has been going on for much longer than it should have, right?" Carlos nodded. "I get it. He's keeping secrets involving his ex, and of course, you're feeling uncertain about your future together."

"Yeah." Carlos turned to face Owen. "I honestly love him, but if he doesn't love me, then we need to end it so we can both move on."

Owen studied the turmoil on Carlos's face. "He loves you. I know he does. You two fight like an old married couple." He smiled. "And you love it. It makes you feel safe and secure. It's that this fight has gone on for much longer than normal and because of what the fight is about."

With a nod, Carlos admitted, "Yeah. Normally, these fights only last a couple of hours to a few days. This one has been going on so long it has me worried."

"Well, it's ending tonight, and he's going to apologize for dragging this out for so long." Owen dropped his hand. "I'll make sure of it."

Carlos snorted. "Cameron apologize? I'll believe it when I see it."

"I'll make you a deal," Owen said slyly. "If he apologizes, you have to give Alex a chance."

Carlos thought about it. "Okay, but Cameron can't know about the deal."

"Deal." Owen stuck out his hand. "And we'll record it."

Taking his hand, Carlos said, "Deal." He eyed Owen. "Even if Cameron doesn't apologize, I'll give Alex a chance. I actually never met him before the hospital. I really wish they caught that bastard that hit him with their car."

"They did." Owen reached past Carlos and opened the door. "It was his bitch mother and sister."

Carlos stood slack-jawed for a moment before following Owen out. "Wait—what!?"

# 34

# AFTER WEDDING ANNOUNCEMENTS

**L**EXI STOOD IN front of everyone gathered in the living room. Alex clutched Owen's hand for dear life. Everyone held flutes of champagne with the exception of Owen and him, who held flutes of sparkling grape juice. She was preparing to make her announcement, and he didn't like the mischievous smirk on Cameron's face.

"You're hurting my hand," Owen whispered to him.

Alex relaxed his grip. "Sorry."

"To the happy couple." Lexi raised her champagne flute. "It's about damn time."

Raising their glasses, everyone cheered, "It's about damn time!"

Everyone drank and Alex smiled, happy that he was here for this happy occasion. That happiness was short-lived when Lexi spoke again.

"Now, I'd like to give the floor to Cameron and Alex." She looked at Carlos pointedly. "I know some of you have been wondering what has been going on with these two, so I'll leave it to them."

Cameron put a hand on Alex's shoulder and whispered, "Showtime."

"Fuck," Alex muttered, letting go of Owen's hand and handing over his drink.

He followed Cameron to stand in front of everyone. Cameron nudged him to speak. "I know," he winced at his voice cracking, "I'm probably the last person any of you want to see here." He held up a hand to stop Hunter from interrupting. "I was an asshole and a jerk to many of you."

He was losing his nerve. He needed Owen. Alex reached out a hand. Owen sat the glasses down on a nearby table and joined him. "After I got hit by that car, I went back home and did some soul searching. This man beside me made me look in the mirror and I didn't like what I saw." He squeezed Owen's hand.

Feeling comforted by Owen standing beside him, Alex continued, "Lexi, Cameron, and Jordan have already accepted my apologies. I hope you all can, too." Alex looked at Dennis. "I never meant to hurt you, Dennis." He looked over at Billy and Carlos. "Billy, I've been a horrible friend to you. Carlos, I know the secret conversations Cameron and I had put a strain on your relationship, but trust me. It was all plutonic." He brought Owen's hand up to his lips and kissed it. "I'm with Owen now."

Cameron cleared his throat. "Owen is the newest member of our team. He and Alex documented their

journey. We're going to put it out there as one of our first shows." Cameron grinned. "Oh, imagine my surprise when I found out Owen is Alex's uncle. Jordan! I believe you're next!"

"Asshole," Alex muttered to Cameron as they exchanged places with Jordan and Billy. People were pelting them with questions that they were ignoring.

Jordan shouted over the commotion. "Guys! Focus! Or I'll have Daniel take a spatula to you all!"

Jordan waited for the laughter to die down before he took Billy's hands in his. "Billy, after I wrote that article about you and the Country Boyz killings, there's been a lot of speculation about what happened to Shadow."

Confused, Billy said, "Yeah, you said you couldn't find him." Billy shrugged. "He simply vanished. No one can find him. We gave up months ago."

"That's because he didn't want to be found," Jordan said nervously. "He still doesn't."

Billy shook his head. "I don't understand what you're saying."

Alex's heart broke when he saw Jordan look at Lexi and then back at Billy. He put his arm around Owen. "This is it," he warned Owen.

"I know." Owen pulled him closer.

With eyes welling with tears, Jordan looked into Billy's eyes. "I know what happened to Shadow. He contacted me and while you were here, I was video-interviewing him. He wanted to share his story in hopes people will finally stop looking for him."

"Where is he? Where is he?" Billy was frantic. His body was starting to tremble with emotion.

Jordan shook his head. "He's living a quiet life now. With his husband. He told me to tell you that he loves you and when he's ready, he'll reach out to you."

"You got to tell me," Billy pleaded, tears trickling down his cheeks

Jordan squeezed his hands. "I wish I could." Jordan pulled Billy into a hug. "I wish I could."

"Let's give them a moment." Lexi motioned everyone to leave. She stopped Alex with a hand on his shoulder. "When Jordan comes out, you go in."

Everyone stood quietly in the kitchen, not knowing what to say until Owen spoke up. "So, I'm Owen, and, yes, technically Alex's uncle and we're dating." All eyes turned to him. He gave a little wave as he pulled Alex close. "I'm his uncle by marriage, not by blood, and no, we didn't meet at the family reunion." He was relieved by the slight chuckle that earned him.

"Owen was my first kiss, my first time, my first boyfriend, my first and last love," Alex added. He saw people whispering among themselves. "No need to whisper. I know it's messed up. When you see the interview I did with Owen and Cameron, you'll see that's just the appetizer."

Carlos tugged Cameron over to him. He exchanged a silent communication with Owen. Owen elbowed Alex. "Get your phone out and record this."

"Okay." Alex brought out his phone and started recording. "Who am I recording?"

"Them," Owen answered. He cleared his throat. "Cameron, don't you think you owe Carlos an apology for what you put him through?"

Cameron looked at Owen in disbelief. "No."

"Cameron," Owen locked eyes with Cameron, "do you love Carlos?"

Cameron didn't hesitate. "Of course I do." He looked at Carlos and saw the uncertainty in his face. "Fuck." He turned to Carlos. "Carlos, I'm sorry for dragging this fight out for so long. I shouldn't have." He took Carlos's hands. "I love you, Latin Lover."

"I love you too, Chipmunk." Carlos pressed his forehead to Cameron's. "I'll work on my jealousy."

Paris commented, "Chipmunk?"

"It's because he wants Carlos's nut between his cheeks," Jordan answered sullenly as he entered the room. "Both sets." Cameron and Owen immediately went to Jordan's side. "He's going to watch the videos. Hopefully, it helps." He let himself be wrapped in Cameron's arms. "I need someone to set my laptop up for him in his room."

Lexi looked at Alex. He nodded. "I'll do it," he volunteered. "It's in the trunk of the rental, right?"

"Yeah, Billy knows the passcode." Jordan wiped away a stray tear. "Thank you."

Alex stepped out to see Billy sitting on the couch with his head in his hands. "Hey, man." He sat beside Billy and put an arm around him. "Let's get you set up in your room to watch these videos, okay?"

"Why won't he tell me?" Billy wept. He let Alex lift him up and toward the hall. "I thought he loved me."

Alex stopped at the first door. "He does love you. He loves you so much he was willing to hurt you to give you what you wanted." He motioned to the door. "Is this your room?"

"Yeah," Billy sniffled. Alex opened the door and led Billy in. Setting him down on the bed, Billy looked at him with glassy eyes. "I can't believe you, of all people, are the one consoling me now."

Alex brushed away a tear from Billy's cheek. "I'm the only person who remotely knows what you're going through." He crouched down. "Owen was my first boyfriend and in order to help me, he had to keep a major secret from me."

"What was it?" Billy asked through choked sobs.

Alex smiled. "He secretly married my uncle to keep my mother from stealing the money he was leaving for me and Owen." Alex shrugged. "So now I'm dating my uncle, sort of."

"That's pretty messed up." Billy laughed through his tears.

Alex nodded. "Yeah, but I didn't know that's why he married my uncle and I hated him because of it. I wouldn't even talk to him so he could tell me." He took Billy's hands. "I lost so much precious time with Owen because I was angry at him." He squeezed Billy's hands. "Don't make the mistake I did. Jordan loves you. He wouldn't be this torn up about this if he didn't."

"I know he loves me," Billy's bottom lip quivered, "but how can he keep this from me?"

Alex gave Billy's hands a reassuring squeeze. "Because it's the only way to give you what you wanted." He stood. "I'm going to grab Jordan's laptop so you can watch the videos and then anything else that you need. Hopefully, then you'll understand why."

"I was planning on asking Jordan to marry me when we got back home," Billy confessed. "I already got his parents' blessing. Carlos and I were going to go ring shopping when we got back. I got us a condo as an engagement present."

Alex cupped Billy's cheek. "You can still do all that." He gave a reassuring smile. "In fact, you will. Now let me go get that laptop, so you hurry up and watch those videos so you can love up on your man."

"Alex," Billy brushed away the falling tears, "thank you."

Alex nodded. "Anytime."

35

# BOYS TALK

**O**WEN SAT ON one side of Jordan and Cameron on the other side of the bed.

"Thank Carlos for letting me have his room here," Jordan said, voice monotone and eyes unable to shed any more tears. "I really appreciate it."

Cameron shoulder bumped him. "Well, I didn't give him much of a choice since I apologized to him. He owes me makeup sex."

"I had Alex record it. I'll have him send it to you." Owen shoulder bumped him from the other side. "Are you going to be okay here by yourself?"

Jordan forced a smile. "Yeah, I need to be close to him in case… in case…" Jordan tried to swallow down the pain. "In case he forgives me."

"He will." Owen put an arm around Jordan's shoulders. "Alex is in there talking with him now. He'll get him to understand why you did what you did."

Cameron slipped an arm around Jordan's waist. "He'll understand. He'll forgive you and then you two can live happily ever after."

"I hope so." Jordan smiled weakly. "If he forgives me, I'll never not show him how much I love him again. I'll appreciate him every single moment of every single day."

Cameron groaned. "You two are going to be insufferable, aren't you?"

"It wouldn't hurt you to do the same for Carlos every once and a while," Jordan shot back. "You can't keep picking fights with him so you two can have makeup sex."

Mock offended, Cameron said, "Excuse me, he's not that innocent. He does the same thing to me."

"Do you see what we have to put up with?" Jordan asked Owen. "Are you sure you want to join this crew?"

Owen answered without hesitation. "Absolutely. Where else am I going to find a group of people okay with me dating my sort of nephew?"

"I think I missed the explanation of that." Jordan cocked his head at Owen. "How about distracting me for a bit by giving me the breakdown of that situation?"

Cameron jumped up. "Let me!" He rubbed his hands together. "Owen was Alex's first kiss, first time, first boyfriend, and his first," he drew out the last word, "loooovvvveeee."

"Jerk." Owen laughed. "Alex's Uncle Terry took me in when my father went to rehab. That's when I met Alex. It was lust at first sight. When I turned eighteen, I married his Uncle Terry. So many complicated

reasons, but we never got to tell Alex before his bitch of a mother found out and turned him against us."

Cameron interrupted, "Side note, his mother and sister were the ones responsible for hitting Alex with the car for the life insurance." Cameron motioned to Owen. "Continue."

"That's pretty much it, besides Alex's mom turning the entire town against me, saying I stole their inheritance, and her ripping people off using crowdfunding for a legal defense that never existed." Owen shrugged. "Oh, and we had to have a police presence at our house because the entire town got pissed at us because everyone renting from us was behind in their rent and we demanded that they get current or evicted because of how they were treating us."

Jordan looked at Owen, stunned. "What?"

"Yeah, it's all sorts of fucked up." Owen smiled at Jordan. "If Alex can forgive me, I'm certain Billy will forgive you."

Cameron blurted out excitedly, "Tell him about your last name!"

"Cameron," Owen groaned.

Jordan prodded, "What about your last name?"

"When it was time to change my last name to help hide things from Alex's mom, Terry put Alex's last name instead of his." Owen's face brightened with a slight smile. "He did it so I didn't have to change my name again for when I married Alex."

Jordan shot a look at Cameron. "You say me and Billy are bad?" He pointed at Owen. "He literally changed his last name to Alex's for when they get married."

"His uncle did that, not me," Owen corrected.

Jordan laughed, "Thank you, guys. This has helped a lot."

"I'm glad." Owen gave him a side hug. "If you want, I can spend the night." He looked at Cameron. "I'm not looking forward to the sounds of makeup sex."

Jordan shook his head. "No. I'm good and I wouldn't want to deprive you of a night of Cameron screaming Carlos's name."

"Payback for me having to listen to you screaming Alex's name last night," Cameron gloated.

There was a knock at the door, then Carlos cautiously came in with Jordan's bag. "Where would you like me to put this?

"Over there." Jordan pointed to the other side of the bed. "Thanks, Carlos."

Carlos sat the bag down. He slipped an arm around Cameron. "Do you want me to talk to Billy before we leave?"

"No." Jordan shook his head. "He's watching the videos now. I don't want to interrupt him. The sooner he's done watching them, the sooner I'll have my answer."

Alex appeared in the doorway. "Is this where the party is?"

"Is he okay?" Jordan asked, fearful of the answer.

Alex moved to stand in front of Jordan. "He will be. Give him time to process everything."

"I guess we should head back to the hotel." Owen stood and put an arm around Alex. "We'll be back first thing in the morning for breakfast, but if you need us before then—"

"I'll call," Jordan finished. "Thank you all so very much. I don't know what I would do without all of you."

Cameron kissed Jordan on the forehead. "Let's never find out, okay?"

# CALL COCK BLOCK

"**T**HIS IS WHERE you recovered?" Owen asked, strolling around Lexi's mansion with Alex.

Alex laughed softly. "Yeah, she's got a nice place, but it was missing one very important thing for me to be happy here."

"What's that?" Owen asked, stepping out onto the patio. "Look at that pool!"

Alex hugged Owen from behind. "You." He kissed Owen on the cheek. "We can go swimming after we unpack if you want."

"Ugh, I didn't bring a swimsuit," Owen moaned. "Why didn't you tell me there was a pool?"

Alex rubbed his crotch against Owen's ass. "Lexi doesn't care if we go nude." He nipped Owen's ear. "Neither do I."

"I wouldn't mind losing my tan lines." Owen turned in Alex's arms. Putting his arms around Alex's neck, he gave him a quick peck on the lips. "I think I'm going to like it out here."

Alex began swaying them. "I'm glad you made me go to the wedding. It was a good start to rebuilding those bridges I burned."

"We would have missed seeing Jordan proposing to Billy, too." Owen began slowly turning them in time with Alex's sways. "I can't believe they asked us to be groomsmen."

Alex leaned in for a kiss, only to be interrupted when their phones started ringing. Pulling away, Alex pulled out his phone and showed Owen the screen. "Cameron."

"Carlos." Owen showed Alex his screen. Answering, he said, "Hello, Carlos."

At the same time, Alex answered his phone. "Hello, Cameron."

They both rolled their eyes as they listened to their respective rants. At the same time, they said, "Hold on," then exchanged phones.

"Cameron, you need to apologize to Carlos," Owen said into the phone. "Yes, it was funny, but it was below the belt to tell Carlos he could be replaced in bed by something you can order off the Internet."

At the same time, Alex said to Carlos, "You are more than a pole and hole. No, he shouldn't have watched ahead in that show you two were watching. Just make him rewatch it with you."

They both rolled their eyes again before saying, "Hold on," and exchanging phones again.

"Carlos, it'll be okay." Owen groaned. "No, don't put on his favorite thong and stretch it out."

To Cameron, Alex said, "Go apologize now, then show him how sorry you are." Alex sighed. "Yes, do it naked."

Together they said, "Goodbye," before simultaneously hanging up.

"I don't remember having these types of conversations with the drones." Alex laughed.

"Drones?" Owen raised an eyebrow. "Who or what are drones?"

"They were the guys I hung out with that sort of orbited around me when I was the hotshot porn guy." Alex groaned at his phone ringing again. "Billy."

"Jordan." Owen held up his ringing phone.

Together they answered, "Hello."

"Yeah, a bed and breakfast sounds like a great idea," Owen said with a smile.

Alex smiled. "Yeah, I think it would be sweet for you to take his last name."

"No, Alex can't help you guys move, but I can." Owen winked at Alex. "After his statement to the police, he has to head back to Springfield to clean up the mess we left behind."

Alex reached out and pulled Owen next to him. "Yes, we'll come over tonight for game night."

"Really? There's another condo getting ready to go on the market in your building?" Owen winked at Alex. "On the other side of Cameron and Carlos?" Alex nodded. "Yeah, we'll take a look at it."

Alex kissed Owen on the forehead. "Yeah, Jordan just told Owen about it. We're going to take a look at it. No promises, though."

"Jordan, we'll talk more about it at game night tonight." Owen hip-bumped Alex. "Yeah, Billy already invited us. See you tonight. Bye."

Alex hip-bumped Owen back. "We'll see you tonight. Bye."

"I know Billy hasn't officially forgiven you," Owen rested his head against Alex's chest, "but I think he has unofficially."

Alex steered them back inside the house. "I think the fact Jordan has helps. I'm glad Dennis didn't hate me for what I did to him."

"Let's go unpack, so we can hit the pool." Owen reached down and grabbed Alex's butt. "I want to see you toast your buns in the sun."

Seductively, Alex said, "Are you going to rub sunscreen on them for me?"

"As long as you repay the favor." Owen gave Alex's butt a firm squeeze. "Lexi said she won't be back for another day or so, right?"

Alex pulled Owen in front of him. "Correct, which means we can be as loud as we want."

# OWEN'S REVENGE

"**T**ONIGHT WAS FUN," Owen said from the bathroom. "I can't believe Jordan and Billy started dating without even realizing they were dating."

Laying on top of the bed naked with his arms behind his bed, Alex shouted back, "I can. Billy is that special kind of silly and goofy, and Jordan seems to compliment that."

"Watching them makes me laugh." Owen stepped into the room naked, hard cock swinging. Alex whistled. "I'm glad you like." He climbed onto the bed and lay beside Alex. "Remind me to thank Lexi for the welcome basket." He leaned down and kissed Alex. "Are you ready for this?"

Alex let out a lecherous growl. "Are you kidding? I get to bottom for my uncle. There are movies made about this."

"Stop it." Owen playfully smacked Alex's chest. "I'm serious."

Alex took Owen's hand and moved it down between his legs. "So am I." He let out a gasp when one of Owen's fingers slipped into his lubed hole. "I prelubed in anticipation of tonight."

"It feels like you prestretched a little too." Owen slipped a second finger in. Alex's body jolted with pleasure. "Looks like I found your spot."

Owen covered Alex's mouth with his. His fingers thrusted in and out of Alex, simultaneously stretching Alex and stroking his pleasure spot as he did so. He slipped a third finger in and moaned with delight at Alex's blissful discomfort. He spread his fingers in Alex, stretching him with the outer two fingers and stroking Alex's spot with the middle.

"Bastard," Alex moaned into the kiss. His cock jumped with every stroke and precum ran like a river onto his stomach. "I want you so badly right now."

Owen growled in Alex's ear, "We've got all night and no one to hear your screams." He ran his tongue over Alex's ear. "I'm going to make sure you're nice and open for when I slide into that tight hole of yours."

"Is this—ugh!" Alex jolted at a bolt of pleasure. "Payback for—Oh, God! The hotel?"

Owen slipped his fingers from Alex. "Maybe." He reached over to Lexi's welcome basket that sat on the nightstand. He pulled out a long, red silk scarf. "Maybe I told Lexi exactly what to put in the basket." He straddled Alex's chest. "Hands above your head."

"Yes, sir." Alex crossed his wrists above his head. Owen looped the scarf through the headboard, then began wrapping one end around one of Alex's wrists and then the other end around the other. "Not too

tight, okay? I want to be able to grab that sweet ass of yours later."

Owen then tied his wrists together. "Such a bossy bottom slut," Owen teased. He pushed his hips forward so his cock brushed Alex's lips. "Open up." With his eyes locked on Alex's, he slid his cock between Alex's hungry lips. "Good boy," he moaned from feeling Alex's warm strong tongue swirling around his crown. "You are one sexy cock sucker, aren't you?"

Owen pushed his cock farther into Alex's mouth until he felt the back of Alex's throat. "Too bad at this angle I can't get it all in." He pulled back, then slid back in. "I can't believe that mouth is going to be all mine to play with from now on." He grabbed the headboard so he could angle his body better. He smiled at Alex's moans.

Owen pumped his cock in and out of Alex's moaning mouth. "Fuck, you're really good at this." He pulled his cock out of Alex's hungry mouth. "Are you trying to make me cum?"

"Just trying to be a good boy," Alex said with a smile. He licked his lips. "Please, sir, may I have some more?"

Owen slipped down to lay his body on his. "Smart ass." He ravaged Alex's mouth with a kiss. His hands roamed along Alex's sides and up across his arms, feeling his hard, defined muscles. He pulled back from the kiss, breathless and eager.

"I hope you're ready." Owen buried his face in Alex's left pit, lapping and flicking his tongue against the sensitive skin and playing with the sparse hair that grew there.

Alex bucked and twisted under Owen's weight. "Bastard!" Alex cried out, before sucking on his lower lip and whimpering, "Owen."

Owen continued his tasting of Alex, moving from his pit to his left nipple. He took the nub between his teeth and chewed gently. "Oh, God! Owen!" Alex tugged on his bonds. Owen flicked his tongue over the nub rapidly. "I'm going to rip this headboard apart!" Alex shouted, tugging on the restraints.

"You can try," Owen said with a casual flick of his tongue, "but then you have to explain to Lexi what happened if you do."

Owen moved to chew on Alex's right nipple while playing with the left nipple with his fingers. "Fuck, that feels good, you asshole!" Owen's right hand moved to stroke the inside of Alex's pit. "Please, don't," Alex managed to get out before Owen abandoned his nipple and started furiously lapping at his pit.

Alex twisted and jerked under Owen. Owen licked up along Alex's biceps, then back down past Alex's pit along the hard lines of his side. He continued toying with Alex's left nipple. He sucked and nibbled on Alex's skin as he made his way over to the center of Alex's hard stomach while Alex moaned and whimpered in pleasure.

"I love the way you squirm under me," Owen teased, running his tongue along the ridges of Alex's stomach. "I wonder how many times I can make you cum tonight."

Alex's voice quivered. "One good time is perfectly acceptable."

"Then I'll have to take my time giving you this one." Owen kissed his way down Alex's stomach, lapping up the pools of precum that gathered in his stomach ridges. "Tasty."

Alex moaned, "It's better fresh from the source."

"Is it?" Owen flicked his tongue over Alex's crown and was rewarded with a moan. "It is."

Owen took the head of Alex's cock and swirled his tongue over the crown. "Stop teasing." Owen released Alex's cock, then kissed his way along Alex's shaft, before licking circles back up to take the crown back in his mouth. "You're so cruel." Owen slowly swallowed Alex's length down while fondling Alex's balls. "Fuck, your mouth feels great."

Owen pulled off to the tip of Alex's cock. He sucked greedily on the tip before releasing it and letting it thump down on Alex's stomach. "Time to really stretch you out." He took hold of Alex's left leg. "On your stomach."

Alex obediently rolled over, twisting the scarf around his wrists tighter. He arched up his ass, letting Owen slip a pillow under him. "You didn't look through this basket, did you?" Owen asked, reaching in and pulling out a small purple vibrator. He flicked it on and it began to vibrate. "Or you did and thought you were going to use these on me." Owen rubbed the vibrating toy along Alex's rim.

"Oh, that feels nice." Alex purred. "I like that." Owen pushed it into Alex, causing him to jolt with surprise, but then he settled back down, enjoying the constant vibration. "Oh, I do like that. We're keeping that." Alex pushed himself up on his elbows. "Fuck.

That's…" he paused to gather his senses. "That's really making me horny."

Owen rotated the toy in Alex. "Is it?" He pushed it in a little deeper and smiled at the groan of ecstasy Alex let out. "How are you doing?"

"Owen," Alex said, his breathing ragged and heavy, "I need your cock in me."

Owen pretended he didn't hear him and continued to stroke Alex's insides with the toy. "What was that? I can't hear you over all this buzzing sound."

"Fuck!" Alex tugged at his bonds. "Owen, fuck me already!"

He playfully tapped Alex's ass. "I still can't hear you."

"Jerk," Alex groaned. Owen tapped his ass playfully again. "Fine," he huffed. He took in a deep breath, then shouted, "Owen! I need your dick in me now!"

Owen pulled the toy from him. "Was that so hard?"

"No, but you better be," Alex snarled, pushing his ass back. "Now get your dick in my ass," he demanded before shouting, "now!"

Owen grabbed Alex by the hips. "You mean this?" He rubbed his cock along Alex's crack.

"Owen," Alex moaned in warning.

He tapped his dick on Alex's hole. "Take a deep breath." He pushed the tip of his cock into Alex with ease. "You okay?"

"Yeah," Alex moaned, pushing back on Owen's cock. "I forgot how good it feels to bottom."

Owen slowly pushed in. "You're so tight and warm around my cock." He sighed. "I could cum by just being in you."

"How about do that after you fucked me senseless?" Alex rocked back and forth. "Damn, your cock feels good."

Owen began rocking his hips back and forth. "Look at us being versatile boys." He took hold of Alex's hips. "You're definitely going to bottom for me more."

"Gladly," Alex growled, rocking back and forth to meet Owen's thrusts.

Owen slapped Alex's ass. "Who knew you'd be such an eager bottom?" He started pounding harder into Alex. "Damn, it feels like you're pulling me in." His hips crashed hard into Alex's ass. "Do you need my dick that damn bad?"

"Yes!" Alex pounded his bound fists into the bed. "I need you to go deeper."

Owen dug his fingers into Alex's hips. "I want to watch your face as I fuck you." Owen pulled out and flipped Alex onto his back. "I need to feel your hands on me." He pulled the scarf and released Alex's hands with a pull. "Fuck, you look sexy."

He hefted Alex's legs onto his shoulders, then leaned forward to skewer Alex with his cock. "Fuck," Alex groaned, wrapping his arms around Owen. "Pound my ass, baby."

With his hands on either side of Alex, Owen kissed him while slowly pumping in and out. "Fuck, you feel so good." He rotated his hips as he sank down into Alex. "So fucking good."

Crushing his mouth to Alex's, Owen began feverishly pounding into Alex. He felt Alex's fingers digging into his back. Owen sucked on Alex's tongue. He could feel the buildup of his orgasm. He pressed

deeper into Alex. His balls began to draw up and felt the tingle in his back.

"Alex!" he cried out into the kiss. He felt his cock pulsing into Alex. He crushed his lips to Alex's. "Oh, baby," he whimpered. "I love you so much right now."

Alex stroked Owen's face. "Of course you do. You just flooded my insides with your genetic material," he teased. "I can still feel your cock pulsing in me."

Owen kissed him. "I don't want to pull out." He kissed Alex again. "I want to stay in you and fuck you until we've both passed out."

"Selfish top," Alex teased. "Don't I get to have an orgasm?"

Owen pretended to think. "Nope." He pumped his hips one more time. "All the orgasms are mine."

"Jerk." Alex maneuvered his legs off Owen's shoulders to wrap around his waist. "Wait until it's my turn to tie you up."

Owen kissed him. "I can't wait." He rolled them over so Alex was on top. "I want to watch you shoot your load all over me while my dick is in you."

"Yeah?" Alex reached over and grabbed the lube from the nightstand. Sitting up, he took his cock in one hand and drizzled lube over his cock as he stroked. "You want to watch me, baby?" Alex capped the lube, then set it aside. "You want me to blow my load all over you?" He rose and fell on Owen's softening cock.

Owen ran his hand up and down Alex's legs and along his sides. "Yeah, Alex. I want to feel your load all over me." Owen could feel his cock hardening again. "Do you want me to shoot another load up you?"

"I'll take it all, baby." Alex could feel his balls churning. "I can feel you getting harder in me." He reached down with his free hand and twisted Owen's right nipple. "I want to cum with you."

Owen started thrusting up into Alex. "I can't believe I'm so close already." He took hold of Alex's hips and pulled him down onto his cock. "You're still so tight and warm."

"Your dick feels so good in me," Alex moaned, tossing his head back. "Owen, I need to cum. Tell me you're close so I can cum."

Owen began pistoning into Alex. "Go ahead, baby. Blow your load."

"Owen!" Alex shouted, arching back and splatting his seed all over Owen's chest and stomach.

The sudden vice grip tightness sent Owen over the edge. He pulled Alex down hard onto him, screaming, "Fuck! Alex!"

The two trembled as their orgasms took over their bodies. Owen dragged his nails along Alex's thighs, leaving marks in their wake. Alex pitched forward, his mouth colliding clumsily with Owen's. Their fevered kiss slowly cooled, and Owen eventually slipped from Alex.

"We need a shower," Alex said between kisses.

Owen held Alex tight. "Ten more years of this first."

"You know, the shower is built for two or more," Alex tempted. "And we're not paying the water bill here."

Owen grinned. "You'll have to top." He wiggled his hips under Alex. "I think my dick is worn out."

"Deal." Alex slipped off Owen and stood. "Come on." He offered his hand to Owen. "You know, I think Jordan has the right idea."

Owen took his hand and allowed himself to be pulled up into Alex's arms. "Oh? About what?"

"He plans on showing Billy he loves him every day." Alex held Owen tight against him. "I plan to do the same for you."

Owen squeezed Alex back. "And I'll do the same for you. Now let's go get cleaned up. We have a future to build together."

## The End

It is with a heavy heart that I am ending this series with this last and final book. Through this series, I have grown so much and I have grown to love the characters. While this is the end of this series, I do not believe this is the last you will see of them.

# BOOK CLUB QUESTIONS

1.  Why do you think Alex can't see the truth about his mother until Owen confronts him with it?

2.  If you were Cameron, would you be so forgiving of your ex-fiancé for cheating?

3.  Why do you think Owen put his dreams on hold to fulfill Terry's wishes?

4.  Despite everything being done legally, why do you think the people of the town were so easily swayed to turn on Owen?

5.  Do you think Danielle ever cared for Alex? For Krystal?

6.  Owen had to keep a major secret that would hurt Alex if he found out. Could you do the same in his situation?

7. Owen and Alex discuss the possibility of having children. Do you think this is an important discussion partners should have?

8. Alex decides to leave the adult film industry. Do you think it was because of his previous infidelity or another reason?

9. Alex was scared to see Owen. Why do you think that was?

10. Owen seemed to draw strength from Alex, like the scene in the tavern. Why do you think that is?

## BIO

ROBERT "ROBBY" J. Lewis is based out of Charleston, South Carolina. He brought you not only the *Shadow Guardian* series but also the *Someone* Series under Robert Lewis. Under Robby Lewis, he has written numerous steamy film scripts for Noir Male, Icon Male, and Luxxxe Studios. He is a social media exclusive for Luxxxe Studios as their Luxxxe Studios Insider and is contracted to write several upcoming steamy movie series. He has been featured in articles on GayVN and JRL Charts. In 2024, he became the first-ever red carpet correspondent for the illustrious Grabby America Award Show. You can keep up with Robert "Robby" J. Lewis's latest releases, news, and antics via his social media or at

www.robert-j-lewis.com.

# Discover more at
# 4HorsemenPublications.com

**10% off using HORSEMEN10**